# DR. TROUBLE

A SUSPENSEFUL ENEMIES TO LOVERS ROMANCE

JENNA GUNN

Copyright © 2022 by Jenna Gunn

All rights reserved.

No part of this book may be reproduced in any form or by any electronic or mechanical means, including information storage and retrieval systems, without written permission from the author, except for the use of brief quotations in a book review.

This book is a work of fiction. Any representations of people, places, or things are merely coincidental.

This book is an Amazon Exclusive book published by Jenna Gunn. If you got this book on any other book site, then you have downloaded an illegal copy. You can be prosecuted. If you find this book free on book websites, please share those with the author because that is illegal use of her content, and can impact the copyright of her book. Your help in fighting illegal book distribution helps protect independent authors and support their future in publishing.

## ABOUT THE AUTHOR

Jenna Gunn is an Amazon Best Selling Author with over 20 published titles. She writes high heat, action, suspense romances with fun, unexpected plots.

Jenna loves badass men, strong women, and enchanting happy ever afters.

Her books explore real word subjects like family relationships, past traumas, disabilities, learning to trust, and the power of growth when we find the mates who see us for who we really can be.

Jenna has also written professionally in education and non-fiction. She's always loved reading romance and began writing romance stories over a decade ago. With a busy career, she didn't pursue publishing, but she took the leap to self-publishing in 2020 and hasn't looked back since.

An adventurous spirit, Jenna is a lover of travel, outdoor fun, and meeting fascinating humans and animals. She lives where the waves break and the snow falls with her husband and Jack Russell fur baby. She's an avid surfer and skier who fills her indoor time with creating new recipes, writing, and reading.

Jenna would love to hear from you and share new releases, book sales, bonus chapters, and free books.

Join her newsletter HERE Get text message updates by texting the word **ALPHAS** to **855-256-3324**

## GRATITUDES

Every book takes a village to write. I'd first like to say thank you to my badass Czech friend who always inspires me with her courage, her wisdom, and her feisty spirit. She shared much with me about culture, language, and the heritage of her home country. I was thrilled at the idea of creating a character that shined a light on an often overlooked corner of the world.

Second, I'd like to thank my dear French friend who always inspires and assists me with all things related to Paris and her native language.

And... huge thank you to my beta readers. You guys are the best. I can't tell you how much our laughs, our discussions, our debates, and our connection means to me. Your expertise helps me accomplish so many things that I never imagined possible. I'm truly blessed to be surrounded by such amazing help.

Many thanks to my editor who always knows what I'm trying to say, even if I make a mess out of it! Thank you for making sure everything is ready for the world and your beautiful words of encouragement in the most challenging hours of bringing a book to life.

And last, but definitely not least, thank you to my rock, my amazing husband. You take me on so many amazing adventures and fill my heart with inspiration and hope every day.

## ABOUT DR. TROUBLE

***Dr. Jameson Scott.***
***Infuriating.***
***Devastating.***
***And everything Simona didn't want to be around.***

Only she had to eat her words when he saved her life.

With eyes that melt ... well, everything. Arms stacked with muscle. A southern drawl that rivals McConaughey.

He's had it all, including what other women might call charm.

But the former spy thought she was immune. If only the man's didn't seem to always show up at just the right time.

Even if that meant following her halfway around the world.

And when her hunt to solve the mystery from her dark past turned dangerous, Scotch put his life on the line.

Simona knows that giving into what her heart wants might mean giving up the only thing she knows is safe. Trusting no one.

Did he save her life because she's worth more alive than dead? Or is he the one man who will end her life of loneliness?

**Dr. Trouble** is a steamy military, medical, suspense romance with explosive heat, exciting action, plot twists, and a big HEA. This book is part of the Agile Security & Rescue series (Book 2) or can be read completely as a stand alone. No cheating or cliffhangers. This is Scotch & Simona's story and if you've read Soldier and the Eden Mountain Firefighters Series you'll recognize them.

Jenna Gunn is a master of suspense, action, and sizzling moments that will turn up the heat on a cold winter night. Her books always feature strong heroes and the smart women who win their hearts.

# PROLOGUE

# Simona

Christmas Night

No sooner than the words 'the man's a cocky asshole' leave my mouth, there's a deep, rumbly man-laugh behind me.

Wouldn't it be just my luck if Dr. Jameson Scott, said cocky asshole, was standing behind me listening to my rant. Agile Security and Rescue already has a medic, we don't need to add a Navy trauma surgeon to the team. *Especially* him.

I grimace. Yep. That *would* be my luck.

Everything I said is the truth. I don't want him mucking up something we've already got sorted out. Admittedly, it is biased truth.

I can't stand doctors.

But as luck goes, it is none other than the brown-eyed,

ridiculously tall, arrogant, bossy, stethoscope-wielding piece of work himself.

In a pressed blue dress shirt that hugs his gigantic square shoulders and a pair of well-worn jeans, the man nearly fills the farmhouse den's doorway. *Gah*. Why does he have to look like that?

Good. Annoyingly good.

Confident.

And… like he belongs with our team.

With his heavy arms crossed, drawing the fine fabric of his shirt tight, he's staring right at me. Humor lights his deep brown eyes and spikes my annoyance. "I've been called much worse, doll. Is that all you've got?"

Somewhere in the recess of my crackling brain, I hear Marshall, my boss, say, "Come on in, Scotch."

Doctor Trouble, AKA Jameson Scott, fondly called 'Scotch' by the rest of our small town, drops onto the arm of the sofa. He tips his five o'clock heavy chin toward the other members of the hostage rescue team. "Sorry I was late. I was taking a shift down in the valley. One of the hospital's E.R. docs is having a baby."

Marshall passes him a drink. "No problem. I just thought, since we were all getting together today, we might share some holiday cheer and give you a chance to meet everyone."

"I appreciate the drink after the day I've had. I swear I treated more cases of heartburn than an Emergency Room sees in a year. Anyway, who knows, maybe I won't be such a cocky asshole after a drink."

He actually has the nerve to wink at me!

I have the sudden urge to kick him off the couch with my combat boot, but Marshall gives me a flat look.

Scotch stops with his cup halfway to his mouth. "Still mad at me from that day at the clinic?"

Fury fills my veins with something very close to molten steel. "See? That's what I mean. Isn't that patient-doctor privilege or something like that?"

Scotch turns up his drink. When he sets it down on his thigh, his eyes are challenging, but his laugh is deep and genuine. "I'm sure you told everyone already that I wouldn't let you walk out of the clinic without stitches, didn't you? I can't see you holding back when you're mad."

For a few tense beats, all I can do is stare at him as I plan my revenge. Marshall clears his throat.

Damn if I want to admit it, but finally, I say, "Okay, maybe I did tell them."

He sips off his spiced rum again. Speaking around his grin, he says, "So, what's up with Agile Security and Rescue these days?"

And just like that, the man slides right into the team. And my headache gets as big as that huge pick-up truck he drives.

I'm fuming inside when Scotch rubs his hands together and asks, "So, when do we go?"

Marshall laughs appreciatively. "As soon as we get the call."

## CHAPTER ONE

*Scotch*

One Month Later

San Miguel is the kind of country that operatives either love or hate. Dirty. War torn. Streets teeming with people and narrow alleys full of dark shadows.

It's nothing to see speeding cars and guns in the hardscrabble capital city of Selva Oscura, so we fit right in. Tearing through traffic, in body armor, loaded to the teeth with weapons in a battered, rented SUV.

Jamming on the brakes, Andre barely misses a scooter with a muttered curse, then guns the gas again. We all know the clock is ticking. Our window for rescuing our target is tight.

Lurching into a pothole, our vehicle sways and I come

dangerously close to bumping into the operator to the left of me. Which might be a shootable offense in her book.

*Simona.*

One name. One expression.

A look that screams 'don't fuck with me'. Which I find both mildly amusing and very interesting.

And did I mention she's hot?

Exotic and beautiful. With her Czech accented English, her pale, almost white blonde hair, and her lush, kissable lips, she makes a hard to miss package.

From the very first time she stepped into the clinic with a deep knife cut on her hand, she had my body on high alert. And knowing she was in my small town put my head on a swivel. Even though her hotness is something I probably should forget. Permanently.

As much as I'd like a romp in the proverbial hay with Simona, she's obviously not interested. Unless it involves lighting me on fire or feeding me to hungry wolves. And me, I'm not even sure what the hell I'm up to since getting out of the Navy.

But my reproductive drive says otherwise. Yes. Yes. Yes, thrums in my veins when anything Simona comes up on radar.

When I glance her way, those incredible eyes of hers are locked on me. Two sighted weapons. Pale blue. Deadly.

Guess I set my fate when I wouldn't let her leave the clinic that night without stitches.

I wish that look didn't make my blood hum and my cock jump.

Now is not the time to get distracted by thoughts of stripping all of her clothes off and kissing that snarl right off her mouth.

We've got a job to do.

## CHAPTER 1

But I can't hold back the low laugh in my chest as I watch her look me over with disdain. "Sugar, you'd burn me to charcoal with that look if you could."

Pressing her peach-pink lips flat with considerable effort, she glares. Planning my demise, I suspect. It would probably make her day, hell, maybe even her year, if I combusted on the spot.

"Try not to shoot me in there," I say with a dark grin.

Good thing I'm wearing a bulletproof vest or she might just make that silent threat a not so silent bullet to my chest.

"Stay out of my way, then," she snaps as she checks her clip for ammo and slams it back into her pistol one more time.

"You always so angry, Sprite? It's really not healthy to carry that kind of energy around, you know?" I purposefully use the nickname I know she hates, just for the fun of teasing her.

Her eyes go wide, then turn into furious slits. "I said, DO NOT call me Sprite."

Damn if she isn't hot as hell when she's like that. All bristly like a wildcat. I bet she'd claw the hell out of me if I got her off.

I'm grinning, with a barrage of dirty thoughts in my head, as I grab the oh shit handle over the SUV's window. We take a tight curve like we're in an Indy car race.

She glares and mutters something in her native tongue as she barely escapes getting thrown into my lap.

I laugh some more. Even though I wouldn't be laughing if she did land on me. I'd probably be growling.

She straightens herself in the seat and snarls.

I shrug a shoulder. "I didn't do it. Mario Andretti up there is the one with the gas pedal."

Andre's behind the wheel. Marshall, the boss man,

shifts in the passenger seat, causing the leather to creak as he adjusts his shoulders. The man's a tank. And as serious as one too. He flicks his wrist and checks his watch again. "Four minutes out."

As the minutes tick down, the air around us begins to crackle with tension. The teasing mood vanishing. Shit's about to get real.

The road noise is the only sound in the SUV. Until the Sat phone rings.

"Talk," Marshall says.

As we listen to his side of the call, I twist my neck, cracking the tension out of it. Since I was a teen, that's how I get my game face wired.

Simona drops her voice, and with a satisfied sound, says, "I knew you'd be scared. You can back out now and make my day."

Yeah. Right.

I lean down slowly and put my mouth right by her ear. "When I crack my neck, it's because I'm ready. And you better be over your shit in about two minutes because we need to be a team when we go in there to rescue that girl. Remember how this works?"

She turns her head away from me. "I hate doctors. You're all assholes."

I unholster my pistol and check the clip. "Handy assholes. But yeah, a lot of us are assholes. I like to think I'm only 50%."

She's not impressed. Which I expected. Simona's had it out for me ever since the clinic. Then she heard I was joining the team for some special operations and she went full on attack mode. All, supposedly, because I have M.D. on my diploma.

# CHAPTER 1

What she doesn't know is that I've always liked a challenge.

That's where I thrive.

Making her like me is going to be fun.

Making her want me would be even more rewarding.

When our driver slams to a stop in the littered alley that's no wider than the SUV, Marshall holds up his hand. We watch and wait for the go signal as the air in the car goes full on electric.

I will give Simona credit, though. She's calm.

Focused.

Her breathing is steady and deep. It's very clear that she's seen some action in her days too. Another thing that attracts the hell out of me.

But that's for another time. If we don't die. Which can happen any time you extract a high value target from an abductor.

Marshall gives us the signal and we slide silently from the car, falling into formation behind him.

The alley grows narrower. The sides climb high above, crisscrossed with rusty fire escapes and tiny dilapidated balconies.

Carefully, we navigate the trash and discarded car parts. I nearly run smack into a chicken when it flutters up from behind a box, screeching.

This is our way in, but thank fuck it's not our way out. The other alley is shorter. Wider and clear enough for the van that's waiting for us to approach the warehouse door we'll be exiting.

Marshall's voice comes over the comm system in my ear. "Extraction vehicles in place?"

Roark, Mako, and Andre check in from their posts. One

above us on a balcony. One in the van. One in the SUV we just left.

The boss man stops, presses his big frame against the wall just outside of a door. Simona, crouching low, takes her spot on the other side of the door.

"We go on one."

"Copy."

Simona quietly echoes her reply.

Marshall counts down, "Three, two, one."

The heel of his boot crushes the lock. With a deafening slam, the door flings inward.

We surge into the dimly lit space. An instant later, we're in a firefight.

Bullets explode around me as the acrid odor of gunpowder fills the air. Everything slows. The movements. The sound of my own breathing in my ears.

A pallet of boxes gives me cover. Marshall rises up and fires a volley of rounds.

And... fuck!

Simona takes off at a run toward the room where we know the target is being held. The girl's got balls. I'll give her that.

But Jesus. What the hell is she thinking?

While Marshall fires again, I sprint after her. My throat tight, my gut cold, and my gun raised.

But a man in all black tactical gear steps out of the room where the girl was supposedly being held. He cuts off our path with a gun pointed right at Simona's face.

The small, unconscious body of a young girl is draped over his broad shoulder. Her bare, pale feet dangle at his waist, hanging below a drab gray sheet. She's breathing. Slowly and steadily. Probably drugged.

# CHAPTER 1

Simona skids to a stop, but lifts her gun. She points it right back at the man's head.

His eyes cut to me before swinging quickly to her. "Move and I'll shoot her in the face."

I hold perfectly still, calculating how I'm going to disarm the bastard. He's thin and wiry. His hold on the pistol is confident. The blackness of the man's eyes would be striking if you liked pit vipers.

I happen to hate snakes.

A vile laugh peels out of the fucker's sneered lips. "Well, well. I never would have thought *you* would be here. It's been a long time, ghost."

Then he fires.

One shot.

A nine-millimeter round.

And Simona falls.

Blood sprays across my face.

The coppery tang fills my nose as I draw a shocked breath.

He steps backward, holding his gun on me now. "Follow me and I'll do the same to the girl."

Simona groans, but I don't look.

Through the comm gear in my ear, Marshall's voice sounds distant. "Get Sprite the fuck out of there. I've got the bastard."

Without lowering my gun, or taking my eyes off the man that I'm going to hunt and kill, slowly, with a scalpel, I grab Simona by the strap of her bulletproof vest.

She weighs nothing as I jerk her up, and loop her in the bend of my arm. Slippery blood, warm and ominous, runs down my wrist as I retreat. And a thousand memories of wounded soldiers stir to life in the back of my mind.

They're always there, just below the surface. Waiting to remind me of the vulnerability and cruelty of humankind.

As I run, I'm yelling in my mic, "Extract us, now!"

"SUV on standby location 2," says Andre.

The warehouse fills with gunshots and stampeding feet, shouting voices in Spanish, but my only focus is on the woman I'm carrying.

Using the planned escape route, I burst into the alley.

Everything is a blur for the next ten seconds.

I shove Simona's shaking body into the back floorboard of the car on her back. I push her knees up which will help her blood pressure and make room so I can fit in the space with her.

The driver screams, "We've got trouble!"

As I slam the door, I'm praying we can get away. The last thing we need is more destruction. "Go! Go! Go!"

Andre hits the gas. We bolt away from the curb as I press my body over Simona's. Shots splinter the rear window.

## CHAPTER TWO

### Scotch

Mother of insanity! I've been in a firefight or two before, but never with so little support. Never in a civilian vehicle on the run from an unknown, unseen enemy.

When the volley of fire stops, Simona's eyes are wide, flying around the windows and back to me. The vehicle skids around another turn. We barely move because we're wedged into the tight as hell space on the back floorboard.

"We're clear. They didn't give much of a chase," Andre yells over the roaring engine.

"That's the only positive thing in this craziness."

Simona's gaze suddenly freezes on me. Focusing in on the blood that sprayed all over me. "Oh god, that looks bad," she says, her voice quivering.

Reaching out with pale fingers, she grips onto my arm and tries to raise her head to look at her injury. Her breath hitches when she sees that my right arm and hand are covered in blood too. A keening comes from her throat.

That sound nearly tears me in half.

I want to stop time. Rewind. Undo the horrible damage the bullet did to her small body. I want to break the fucker in half. Carve him up bit by bit.

Radio chatter breaks in over the comm system. I rip hers off of her ear. She doesn't need to hear that shit.

The only thing that matters right now is right here. Her and me.

Hoarsely, she says, "That... wasn't supposed to happen." A tear leaks from her eye, traces across her cheek, across the small moon shaped birthmark, down into her blonde braid.

With a quivering voice, she says, "I'm angry as hell to admit this, but I'm scared."

Her skin is cool and damp when I cup her face with my free hand. "It's okay, Sprite. I've got you. Look at me."

The pale blue of her eyes is filled with a war of fear and resolve. Emotions and pain ghost across her face.

It guts me. I've seen a lot of terrible crap. But for some reason, seeing her frightened, in pain, does something visceral to me.

That rattles me too.

I'm no greenhorn at seeing broken bodies.

Leaning down, I get right in her face. Eye to eye. "I'm right here. I won't leave you. Okay?"

She nods, whispers, "I've never been shot."

"It hurts. I have. I can't give you anything for pain right now."

She gasps when we hit a hard bump. After she catches her breath, she says words that change everything. "I'm allergic to opioids. That's why I didn't get numbing when you gave me stitches at the clinic."

## CHAPTER 2

My breath locks up hard. This is really bad news. "Fuck, you should have told me to have something else on hand..."

Clenching my jaw, I try to get my head around that royally fucked up announcement. Things just went from bad to nightmarish.

On a hissed breath, through clenched teeth, Simona says, "I didn't think I was going to get shot. I've been shot at plenty. But I didn't think it would happen."

My skin bristles with anger. I should have known this. Without knowing, I can't take proper care of her. "And how long have you been in the business of slinging guns?"

She ignores my question. After a beat, she says, "I've got a thing about blood. Especially my own blood."

Hoping I can make her feel a little more at ease, I say, "Not me. Doesn't bother me at all." I compress her arm tighter against the temporary bandage, doing my damndest to cut off the blood flow.

"That's a *lot* of blood."

I'd be scared all to hell if it was me laying on the floorboard gushing blood too. Jesus. All I want to do is hold her tight against me, kiss the hell out of her, and tell her everything is going to be alright.

No way am I going to tell her how fucked up this situation really is. There's no use scaring her more. "I've got you." I repeat as I stick her slender forearm with the IV from my pack. "This is what I do. I've saved hundreds of people from bullet wounds."

She nods as her chest rises and falls in shaky bursts. Her face is tight with pain.

"Can you use a tourniquet?"

"Too high for a tourniquet, but I know what to do."

Trembling, she says, "Are you sure?"

"I'm a Navy trauma surgeon. And I'm your only bet right now."

She tries to smile, but she winces instead. "Oh well, then, if you're all I've got."

The entry point is just lateral to the axilla, deep in her upper arm, but as far as I can tell it missed hitting bone, and went all the way through. But it's bleeding a fuckton. "The bullet did a lot of damage, which I'm sure you know."

She nods. Her whole body is shaking beneath me as I rip out the other medical supplies tucked in my tactical vest.

"Andre, ETA to the hospital?"

"Just over five minutes."

Hardening my voice, I say, "We got this. You hear me?"

Andre brakes hard and the car shudders. Growling, I shift, and reposition my 6'4 frame into the tight as hell space, leaning over her with my thigh shoved between her legs.

If I could get Simona to a place where I could work on the wound, I could do a lot more to stop the bleeding, but that's not happening in this car. I can barely fit.

I press harder. She concentrates on breathing.

"That's it. Stay with me."

She nods, jerkily. "I'm trying."

Andre calls, "Three minutes."

"Three minutes..." she repeats. The threadiness of her voice scares the damned life out of me.

I try to engage her. Keep her present. "Who was he?"

She narrows her eyes. "Pavel. He's trash. A half-assed spy wannabe. Someone I knew a long time ago."

"He's mine," I reply, letting venom fill my voice. "When this is done, I'm going to make him pay for this."

I squeeze the clear IV bag, pushing more fluids into her.

## CHAPTER 2

Her fingers flex against my arm, chilled now where they press against my heated skin.

"I'm cold."

"I know, babe. We're almost there."

If only it wasn't going to be a dirty, third world hospital.

I'm worried as hell about what we are going to find. Real fear grips my lungs.

I have to remind myself that plenty of lives have been saved in nasty places. I know because I've been there. In the armpits of the world for nearly 15 years. Doing my best to be the doctor my father said I'd never be.

The damaged road vibrates us so hard the car groans. And the whole way, I wonder how they'll react at that hospital when I tell them I'm going to stand in on the surgery Simona's going to need to save her life.

Because I'm not letting anyone else ruin her chances at living.

# CHAPTER THREE

# Simona

I should have paid more attention to those Spanish lessons I took online a few years ago. Because I can't understand a damned word that Scotch and Andre are yelling.

At least someone studied, apparently. Scotch, with the thick cords in his neck standing out, is screaming at someone as fluently as if he was a native speaker. And Andre isn't missing a beat either.

Everyone's yelling in a violent clash of words that I've never heard, as Scotch shoves his way through the emergency room with me clutched against his chest. All while holding pressure on my wound.

"Guess you're the right guy for the job," I say as I drop my head to his thick shoulder. Not that I have much choice. I'm weak as an overdone spaghetti noodle. And he feels safe. Strong. Vital. Everything I need. "I can't speak Spanish. Well, I can, but it takes forever. It's nothing like Slavic languages."

He doesn't reply. He's busy storming down the corridor, barking orders or something, using words that make no sense to me. But for some reason, talking at him feels better. Because it's helping me stay awake, when all I want to do is curl into him and get warm and go to sleep.

My eyes whip open.

*No.*

No sleep!

I'm not ready for the dirt nap. I've got things to do. And dying isn't one of them.

"Scotch, is someone going to fix me soon?"

He shoves through a set of silver metal swinging doors. "Yep."

"Oh, god! Is this an operating room?"

"It's going to be."

That's the last thing I remember before everything fades to black.

* * *

WHAT IS THAT SOUND?

Beep. Beep. Beep.

On and on.

Someone *please* stop that noise before I break something.

If only I could lift my arms. They must weigh ten thousand pounds.

Beep. Beep. Beep. Beep.

I turn my head to the side and wince. Ugh. *Damn.* I thought the pain would be gone.

But it's not. Blinking my scratchy eyes, I scan over the

room. It's small, stark white, and smells mildly of antiseptic. Better than I expected for San Miguel.

"You're awake."

I jolt at the sound of the deep, smoky, southern voice from my other side.

I know that voice.

Instinctively, I revert to cursing in Czech. *"Do prdele."*

But even as I curse him, my core clenches and fills with warmth. Talk about a mind-fuck.

I turn my head toward *him*.

My vocal cords don't want to work. Yet, I manage one word that sums up so much. "You."

Scotch watches me for a second before he flashes that cocky grin he wears so often. "Yep. You haven't succeeded in getting rid of me yet."

"Damn," I mutter and close my eyes. Carefully, I breathe. Because it hurts like hell to move anything south of my chin.

"How are you feeling?"

I swallow the grit in my mouth. My voice is as hoarse as if I am a hundred years old. "Tired. Thirsty."

When I open my heavy lids again, I see fatigue and worry in his somber expression. "You'll feel a little better with every hour that passes."

I raise a brow in question at him. "Really? Because I think you're overstating."

In that sultry voice of his, he speaks slowly. With meaning. Two words. "Trust me."

Oh. God.

I don't want to.

Not him.

But I can't really deny that I do. Because I am here, all thanks to him sticking his fingers inside the bullet wound to

## CHAPTER 3

staunch the life that was pouring out of me all over the back floor of that car.

In some part of my brain, way back behind my defenses, I know I'm forever bound to the man for that.

Forever.

As Prince's song said... "that's a mighty long time."

We hold eyes for a few seconds before his grin softens into a warm smile.

Mother of God. Does he have to look like that?

All five o'clock shadow, square strong jaw, and dark, devouring eyes. How can the man look so good after going through hell?

Oh, wait. I'm the one who went through hell.

I let out a painful huff. "What are you smiling about?"

Scotch, AKA Jameson Scott, M.D., shakes his head once. "All of those emotions that just went across your face ended with one that looks a lot like admission."

I bristle. God, he's annoying.

In my croaky voice, I ask, "And what would I be admitting?"

He almost looks... pleased. "That you do trust me."

I shift in the bed, which makes me wince and suck in a sharp breath. Just the slightest attempt to move upward on the pillow and I'm shaking with pain. Scotch is on his feet, instantly. Standing to his full, imposing height. "Don't. Let me help."

Sliding one of his gigantic paws under my other arm, he easily lifts me higher on the pillow. His hand curves along the bare skin of my chest thanks to the floppy hospital gown.

Electrical zingers shoot out from the place where his hand is against me.

He makes a sound of approval deep in his chest.

"There. Try not to lift yourself." His breath stirs my hair and sends a blistering awareness down my neck.

I nod because my voice is now gone. GONE.

When I expect him to move back, he reaches up and sets the back of his hand against my forehead.

My heart thuds as he just holds it there. Then he slides his fingers into my hair. A move so clinical, yet so intimate, that there's a thundering race going on inside my chest.

"You're a little warm for my taste."

Yeah. *You think?*

Mister, maybe it has something to do with those incredible biceps showing below your t-shirt—

Or the perfect soft contour of your masculine lips.

Or the way your deep, soulful, cocoa brown eyes hold me captive.

So, yes. I am hot.

Which annoys the hell out of me.

"It's nothing," I mutter.

One side of his mouth pinches. "I'm going to have some blood drawn." Moving to the sink, he washes his hands. And I can't peel my eyes off the strong vee of his back in his black t-shirt and the tight curve of his muscular lower body in his black tactical cargo pants.

I rip my eyes away when he turns around. But he comes right at me with that damn disarming look of concern on his face. When he leans over the bed and reaches for the corner of my gown, I gasp. "Hey! What do you think you're doing?"

As if it's the most obvious thing in the world, he says, "Checking your dressing."

I grab his wrist. "Uh, I'm... at least I think I am, naked under there."

## CHAPTER 3

Slowly, his eyes trace over my face, then hold on my lips. "Yes. You are."

"Oh god. Don't tell me you saw me... naked."

He plants his hand next to my head on the bed. "I've seen you stare down a man pointing a gun right in your face without so much as a flinch. There's no way you're afraid to be seen naked."

I can barely look at him. Oh god. The way he looks at me, like he's seeing something that I don't want him to see.

"That's different."

He takes my face in his warm, strong hand and tilts it up. "Look, I'm a doctor. I am the person that cut you out of your clothes. I prepped you for surgery. I worked on you for two hours to fix the holes that bullet left. So, yes. I've seen you naked. But I promise you this, you were respected, and I hear you."

Every emotion inside my chest clogs up my throat all at once.

What's happening to me?

I do not know these emotions.

My head spins as I try to get my foggy brain cells around all of the words that just came out of his beautiful mouth. Heavy words like surgery and respected.

"You—you did the surgery?"

Tracing his thumb over my cheek, he lets out a quick punctuating breath. His expression hardens, and those dark eyes turn even stormier. "Yeah. When I found out how inexperienced the surgeon was, I kicked his ass out of the operating suite."

Lord. This man. Is there anything he can't do?

I surprise myself when I smile. "I'm just picturing you pointing a gun at some guy in scrubs."

But Scotch doesn't smile. "Security didn't like it one bit,

but I told them to fuck off or I'd shoot the guy so he couldn't operate on anyone."

I'm so shocked I can't move or breathe.

He leans down, and that's the moment I know I'm in real trouble, because the man who just threatened to kill a surgeon over my safety is going to kiss me.

And I'm powerless against the feeling inside of my chest. And the way I feel like I'm spiraling as the space between us heats with electric energy.

My body goes hot, then cold, then hot again in a flash.

He's going to kiss *me*!

I'm shaky with anticipation and completely baffled when he leans down and presses his forehead against mine.

His breathing is as ragged as mine.

And I almost scream.

He was supposed to kiss me!

"What's wrong?" I blurt.

He growls as his hand cradles my head in his big palm. "Jesus." He draws in a deep breath. "You just woke up from anesthesia after major surgery. One of us needs to be thinking with a clear head here. And the head I'm thinking with is the last one either of us should trust."

I twist my fingers into his t-shirt. "I'm going to shoot you when you give me my gun back."

His mouth pulls tight. "About that..."

I gasp and snap, "Where's my gun?"

"Not here."

I close my eyes and count to ten. Twice. "You're kidding me, right?"

He chuckles darkly. "I wish I was."

I shove at him. Then curse the pain that shoots through my shoulder. "That was my favorite nine mil."

Gently, Scotch pries my fingers off of his shirt. "They

make more every day. I had one thing on my mind when you were shot. Saving your life, even though you had one thing in mind since we met."

"What's that?" I say half grumbling.

"Making me your enemy."

I just glare at him. He's right. I wanted nothing more than to go head-to-head with him. I just didn't know it was head-to-head like this, where all I want is to know how that hard mouth of his will feel against mine.

He picks up his Agile team baseball cap off the table. "I'll be back. I'm going to order the blood tests. Stay out of trouble while I'm gone."

I don't bother looking when he walks out the door because I know my traitorous eyes would do nothing but look at his much too hot ass.

## CHAPTER FOUR

*Scotch*

I almost kissed her.

Fuck. Me.

What the hell?

Oh, sure, I want to kiss her. Like no other woman I've ever wanted. That's not the point of debate. My timing, on the other hand, is seriously bad. As in deplorable.

It's the exhaustion. It has to be.

*Lie to yourself some more, buddy.*

Ack! Suddenly, I feel like punching something. Everything. Including my dick into her sweet little body. But think better of hitting the wall outside her hospital room. A broken hand is the last thing I need right now.

Andre stands up from the stool he's half perched on across the hallway. "How is she?"

"Awake. Alert. I'm ordering some tests."

# CHAPTER 4

His face is tight with worry. The same that's tying up my gut in a knot. We *do not* need to be in San Miguel.

He nods, "We need to mobilize soon."

"I know. Once I get the labs, I'll know more. I hope we can move out soon."

"Marshall's going to turn the plane back around as soon as they are stateside."

"Is the safe house still a green light?"

"Affirmative."

"How's target?"

"As good as can be. Recovering. Eating. They gave her fluids on the plane. Cole, as you know, is a medic, so he had it all under control."

"Thank fuck. You know, I still can't believe that bastard got away from Marshall."

Andre shakes his head. "Me either. Or that he left the kidnaped girl unattended while he got the airplane out of the hangar."

"It worked out. No more gunfire needed. And the target is safe and on the way home to her family."

I glance toward the nurses' station where a cluster of hospital staff is sneaking looks at us. Dropping my voice, I say, "I'd prefer if we weren't the only two left in the country with her in this state."

Andre taps his fingers on the assault rifle in his arms. "Yep, makes me twitchy."

"Me too. We need a bigger team if we're doing shit like this."

"I'm working on that. I've got some buddies who may come onboard."

"Roger that. Hang tight for a bit longer. We'll get the hell out of here ASAP."

He takes a seat on the stool again, cradling his gun at the

ready in plain sight. No questions about the fact that he'll shoot anything that threatens us.

Andre is solid. Brick skyscraper solid.

But I'd feel a hell of a lot better if there were ten of us.

The nurses, skittish as deer, step back from the desk in unison when I approach. I'm sure they heard what went down when we arrived.

In Spanish, I say, "It's okay. There's nothing to be afraid of."

One woman narrows her eyes on me as two others make a point to stand behind her. In broken English, the woman asks, "What do you want?"

"A temperature check, plus lab tests—CBC, CRP, CMP."

Obviously the brave one of the lot of them, she picks up a basket with supplies off the counter and brushes past me.

I follow her into the private room where Simona is resting. Another thing I demanded. No shared wards.

She sets her supplies on the small table next to the bed. "The doctor wants blood."

I watch over every move she makes, the way she washes her hands and puts on her gloves. The preparation of Simona's arm for the needle. The way she labels the vials of blood.

When the blood's drawn and placed back in the basket, she uses a thermometer to take Simona's temperature.

"He is very smart." The woman nods toward me.

Simona twists her lips to the side in reply.

Ignoring her glare, I ask the nurse, "What's her temperature?"

"One hundred."

"We need to check her blood for signs of infection. I'd

like for you to do a urinalysis also. Make sure I get the results from the lab as soon as possible."

She raises a brow, but replies, "Si."

Simona's watching our exchange, her eyes a little more focused than earlier.

"She's going to collect a urine sample."

Her eyes flare. "You are NOT sticking around for that."

"Fair enough. I'll be outside."

After a few minutes, the nurse leaves and I return to the room to find Simona looking upset.

"What's wrong, babe?"

"Babe?" She huffs. "So, since you're the doctor, I guess I need to tell you. The pain in my shoulder is getting worse."

"It's almost time for another dose of medication."

"What did you give me?"

"Naprosyn."

"English, please. Or Czech would be even better. I know one thing, I'm not getting shot again."

"I'd prefer that. Especially on my watch."

She half grins. "What, did this stress you out?"

I step toward the bed. Being pulled toward her by some magnetic female force. "You stress me out."

Her grin grows as she leans back against the pillow. "Do I?"

"Yes. You do."

"Why's that?"

"Because I vacillate between wanting to kiss you senseless and spank your ass for being such a pain."

She presses her lips flat to hide her smile. And my body hums like an engine waiting to take off from the start line. "You're maddening," I say as I plant my hands on the bed beside her head and lean toward her.

Those icy eyes spark. "Me? You're the problem."

"We may have to arm wrestle over this."

She smirks. "I'd win."

"Hardly. Have you seen the size of my guns?"

That gets a chuckle from her. "Maybe."

Ah, so she does notice me...

My ego thuds a fist against its chest.

Her crystal-clear eyes darken as I grip her chin and tip her face up. Then I do what I told myself I wouldn't. I take her mouth.

Deeply. Forcing her to let me in. Demanding her tongue tangle with mine. Like I have every right to violate her perfect mouth with my demanding thrusts.

I half expect her to bite me. Or slug me in the side of the head with something. What I don't expect is the throaty growl she lets slip from her.

If I wasn't in trouble before. I. Am. Now.

Because she tastes like honey, and fire.

And dark, sinful pleasure.

She meets the kiss head on, just like she did the man with the gun, and matches my invasion, taste for taste. Thrust for thrust.

Suddenly, I'm not sure who owns the kiss. But I don't give a fuck. I'll take everything the fire-breathing vixen wants to dish out.

I like it hot.

The hotter, the better.

A knock sounds on the door. "Doctor!" The nurse breezes in before I can untangle myself from Simona.

"Ohhh. Lo siento."

"No pasa nada," I reply, breathing raggedly.

The nurse clears her throat. "The medication... we have no more."

Gripping the bed railing, I try to get my head back online. "Which one?"

"The pain medication."

"What do you have?"

She rattles off three medications.

"That's it?"

"Si. We have no more. It's very difficult to get medication in San Miguel."

When I glance at Simona, she's flushed and looking a little dazed. "Do you have Lyrica?"

"No. None."

In Spanish, I ask, "What do you give patients who cannot have opioid medication?"

"Nothing," she replies in English.

A choking sound comes from Simona.

Gritting my teeth, I say, "We have a problem."

## CHAPTER FIVE

## Simona

I wretch and shake as the pain sets in, hard. This sucks! Scotch holds my hair back and wipes my face with a cool towel.

God. I hate being sick. It's so... vulnerable.

When the worst of the nausea subsides, I lean back, drained.

Scotch looks distressed as fuck. Like he's about ready to chew through the railing on the side of the hospital bed. His brow heavy as a thundercloud, he says, "I hate to ask you this, but are you ready?"

I swallow the god-awful taste in my mouth. "Do I look flipping ready?"

His eyes soften for a beat before the hardness returns. "That's my girl. Now I know you're okay. When you're angry at me, I feel better."

Wrapping the sheet around my shoulders, he says,

## CHAPTER 5

"There's movement outside the hospital I don't like. There's some kind of coup in the works. We need to get to the safe house, now."

I groan and swing my feet toward the side of the bed. But before I can move very far, he scoops me up in his arms.

"Great. Here we go again," I mutter.

But Scotch doesn't answer. And Andre looks like he's ready to mow someone down if they even throw a glance in his direction.

I close my eyes and fight back screaming in pain as Scotch storms down a corridor and out into a back alley where our SUV is waiting.

It's daylight. And I have no idea what day or time it is. The sweltering heat wraps around us.

Andre closes the car door behind Scotch, then hurtles himself behind the wheel.

When we start bouncing along the road, I can't hold the curses in any longer.

Scotch, pistol gripped in his hand, swivels and scans the windows as Andre flies through the alleys. "You've got the address for the curandero?"

Wiping the cold sweat off my face, I ask, "Is that the medicine person?"

"The local native healer. The nurse said he's the one that will have something to give you for pain." He cuts me a glare, and says, "Don't even say you don't need anything because you do. You wouldn't be vomiting your guts out if you had something."

Through gritted teeth, I say, "I'll live."

"That's the plan."

The road surface changes beneath the car, and for a few moments, I get relief, then it changes to rutted dirt, and the pain increases tenfold.

Panting like I'm giving birth, sweat dripping off my face, I yell at Andre, "You're killing me!"

The man glances in the rearview mirror and back at the road. For some reason, I have a feeling he's seen people in far worse pain than me. He doesn't let up.

After another half-hour of pure hell, he slows the car. Scotch pulls a loose shirt over his body armor as we turn onto an even smaller road. Finally, we come to a makeshift gate made of tree limbs.

"Lay down."

"What?"

"I want your head down, below the glass."

"For Christ's sake, you—"

His gaze is so hard, I know what's coming. Either I lie down or he's going to put me down on the seat. Planning all the ways I'm going to hurt him, I slide down to the floor. "Happy?"

"No." He climbs out of the car, adjusting his ball cap low, shutting the door, leaving Andre and me.

"I'm not licking some frog."

From the front, Andre chuckles. "We'll see about that."

Dropping my head back on the seat, I mutter, "Great. Thanks for taking his side."

Five minutes later, Scotch is climbing back in the car. Andre throws it in reverse and backs out like we're being chased.

Whatever the healer, shaman, medicine person gave Scotch is wrapped in big green leaves. A spicy, earthy scent fills the car. "Do you really know what you're doing?"

"I studied some indigenous medicines. But I'm not the one that matters. That man knows what he's doing."

"Great. I get to be an experiment."

"Honey, I hate to tell you this, but you already were."

# CHAPTER 5

I gape at him. "Let me give you some advice. That's not what you want to say to a patient. Remember the concept of bedside manner?"

When Scotch chuckles, I don't laugh.

"You're not improving my opinion of doctors."

"Wait until I use this stuff on you..."

"Oh, lord. Now I'm really worried."

## CHAPTER SIX

*Scotch*

Carefully, I spread out the medical supplies that I filched from the hospital out on the car seat. I frown as I go through the meager haul. What we have is what I could fit in my cargo pants pockets. "Andre, how long before we can get that flight?"

"Marshall messaged that they just landed in Florida to refuel. Then on to New York to meet the kid's parents."

"Can we get another flight out of here? A commercial one? I'd really feel better if we were back stateside."

"Maybe. I'll check as soon as we land at the safe-house. Is everything okay?"

"I'm going to need some other medical supplies. Some bandages, some antiseptic. Soap. More gloves."

"I'll take you to the safe house and I'll get it. Just write a list."

## CHAPTER 6

Simona's a literal wreck. Her color is pale. The hospital gown hangs from her shoulders. She's hunched in pain. No patient in her shape should be bouncing around in the back of a car.

It damn near rips me to shreds.

Setting the leaf wrapped medicine on the car seat, I say, "This stuff is kind of ugly, be forewarned."

"I don't like the sound of that."

"Appearance isn't the important part."

She scoffs. "I'm pretty sure a man has never said those words before."

"Damn. Not only do I have being a doctor against me, now it's being a man too. I guess I'm screwed."

Narrowing her eyes, she says, "I don't hate all men."

Her blonde brow is arched as she watches me unfold the leaf that's wrapped around the gooey mass. With disgust in her voice, she says, "Is that—"

"Not feces..."

The tension in her face relaxes. "Thank god."

I don't tell her it's been chewed and spit by the medicine man, though. Unless she asks specifically, I'll keep that part to myself.

She grabs her nose. "Eew."

It's strong enough to melt paint. Good paint. The kind they bake onto metal. I chuckle. "Potent."

"I'm going to smell like I've been living in a trench in the jungle."

"Just for a couple days."

"I'm already tired of this. Being an invalid is infuriating. How long before I'm back to normal?"

Drumroll... bad news coming. News I know she's going to freak out about. "Six to twelve weeks."

She groans and stares a hole in me. "You're kidding."

"No, I'm not."

The entire time I apply the gooey medicine using the flat, hand-carved stick the medicine man gave me, Simona fumes. She's so mad that her whole energetic field is vibrating. "I'm going to shoot that son of a bitch. I don't have time to sit around for two months. I need to work. I have rent to pay. And I'll go crazy. I can't sit still for weeks. I've never even taken two weeks off. And that's saying something, because I've been working since I was fourteen."

I let her talk without interrupting. Greedy to learn more about her. Hungry for any morsel she'll give me. Puzzles. Mirrors. Smoke. That's what she is, and I want to see what's behind it all.

There's a crease between her brows as she grumbles, "I can't understand why Pavel shot me. That's what I've been thinking about this whole time. I mean, I guess it could have been to foil our rescue. But he could have shot you."

She winces but goes on. "Of course, he might have known I'd leave you if he shot you. So, he shot me instead."

"Why wouldn't he think I'd leave you?"

She yawns and blinks slowly. A sedate rise and fall of blonde lashes over mesmerizing blue eyes. "You have a medical patch on your tactical vest."

"Damn. I didn't even think about that." The girl is smart. Another thing that stirs me about her.

Her eyes go softer. She stretches her legs beneath the sheet and yawns again. "I'm feeling..."

"Sleepy. That's supposed to happen. How's the pain?"

Her head drops forward. "Huh?"

Shit. She's like a noodle. I lean her over until she's laying on her back with her head on my lap. She blinks deliberately and looks up at me. Grinning. "Awe, aren't you so handsome?"

## CHAPTER 6

Oh hell. She's trashed.

"Look at that jaw. Superman would be jealous of all those hard angles."

Andre glances at me in the rearview. He's smirking. I give him a death glare.

"Will you kiss me again?"

Fuck me. That voice dripping in sexy, hushed desire.

"Uh." I purposefully do not look at Andre. Or think about the hard-on that's inevitable beneath her head. "Why don't you doze?"

"When you were looking at me naked, did you see the tattoo on my—"

"Let's not talk right now."

Fuck! Somebody get me out of this nightmare. Talk about the wrong time. This is *not* going as I hoped.

She starts giggling. "Some doctor you are. Afraid to talk about my labia."

Andre chuckles.

I huff out a grunt. My face is flaming red, has to be, because my shirt is about to ignite. "Go. To. Sleep."

"I feel good. Why should I sleep? I think maybe we should talk about this kiss some more."

She pokes me in the center of my tactical vest with her pointer finger. "Or maybe we should talk about what's in your pants. Do you have a big stethoscope?"

I nearly choke to death on my own saliva. "No. Let's not."

"I thought with the way you kissed me you'd want to show me your—."

Damn woman. "Simona!"

She makes a satisfied sound in her throat as she grins.

I shake my head. Vixen. All attitude and sexy as fuck wrapped up in a tight little package with every damn trait I find irresistible. "Just close your eyes and fall asleep. Your body needs it."

And I need it. God help me.

"I'm aroused. Everything is all warm from my head to my...."

I bite out a growl. *"Faaak—"*

"I can't help it. Is this supposed to happen?"

I remove her finger from my chest and press it down to her side. Touching me is a really bad idea right now. "Hell if I know."

"Put some of that stuff on you."

Andre laughs out loud in the front seat.

"No. Actually, that's a 'hell, no'."

My control is paper thin right now. An aphrodisiac would turn me into a rutting, wild animal.

Her wet-dream inducing lower lip sticks out in a pout. *"The man is a chicken."*

"Call me what you want. I'm not only your doctor, I'm guarding you from that crazy fucker that shot you point blank. I need to have a clear head."

She sighs. "Ah, you do have a point. Maybe later. Maybe you can use it on the way home to the States and we can join the mile high club together."

I drop my head back onto the headrest of the seat. "God. Save. Me. My patient has been possessed."

Eyeballing the salve, I consider slathering another dose on her to knock her out, because the last thing I want to be talking about or thinking about is kissing her.

Mile high clubs.

And god forbid, a tattoo on her *labia!*

## CHAPTER SEVEN

*Scotch*

The bedroom door latch clicks as I pull it closed behind me. "She's asleep."

Andre suppresses his smirk. "That smelly crap flipped her for a loop."

Shaking my head, I mutter, "He warned me."

He eases back the curtain just enough to take a look outside the small window. "She's a handful anyway. Give her drugs and she's a real firecracker."

Dropping onto the sofa, I ask, "What's her story?"

"Your guess is as good as mine. I know she's from the Czech Republic, but she never lets on much. Marshall might know more."

"Any men in the picture?"

"I haven't known her that long, but none since I started with Agile. But honestly, she could be banging the entire

Cowboys football team and no one would know. She's walking smoke and mirrors."

A really big, ugly green monster roars inside of me. "You just gave me indigestion. The kind that Pepcid can't cure."

His eyes swing to mine. "It's true. She's an enigma."

"Aren't we all?"

He shrugs as he goes back to watching the street below. "I guess. But her? She's next level."

"What kind of spook was she?"

"Again, you're asking the wrong guy." He chuckles. "She's under your skin."

I shake my head and blow out a long breath full of frustration for myself. "Unfortunately. Like a splinter."

Everything about the pure lust I have for her is screwed up. A) She's a coworker. B) She's a patient. C) She's got some kind of beef with me.

"I'll make myself scarce if you want to—"

"I'm not fucking her. She just got shot. Did you see how much blood she lost?"

He grunts, "I wasn't sure she'd make it."

Scrubbing my hand over my face, I tell Andre what I'm not sure I'll tell her. "I transfused her with my blood."

He doesn't say anything for a few seconds. Then he nods. "No shit. Now, that's next level."

"They didn't have blood."

"You're a universal donor or a match?"

"Universal donor."

Andre shifts to the other side of the window and scans the street. "I'll remember that."

"Don't get yourself shot, please."

Andre chuckles darkly. "Been there. Done that. But I've never looked down a gun in the face and taken a direct hit."

Propping my foot on the rickety coffee table, I say, "Me either. She's got cojones."

"You don't know the half of it. Sometimes, I wonder if she's got a death wish. Who was that son of a bitch, by the way?"

"Someone from her past, according to her."

He bristles and instantly asks, "Lover?"

"I wondered that myself. Something that's bothering me... he did not shoot to kill. Or he's the worst shot in the history of man."

"What the hell, then?"

"My question exactly."

## CHAPTER EIGHT

## Simona

Wow. I'm all warm and yummy feeling inside. Amen for tribal medicine. If only it didn't smell like pond scum. But my pain is minimal. And I'm on a nice little cloud. So much better than I was. Which is the reason I crawl out of bed to get myself cleaned up.

Slowly, I test my feet. The floor feels stable. Okay, good so far. I'm weak but upright. I take a couple of steps. Not exactly drunk, but a little wobbly, maybe it's all the blood I lost.

The next two steps go pretty well. But the third... not so much. Reaching for the dresser, I catch my balance.

So... okay, maybe I'm not too steady.

But I don't have far to go. I can crawl if I have to. Leaning heavily on this and that, first the furniture, then the wall, I make my way to the small bathroom.

The space is tidy, narrow, and painted light blue. An

## CHAPTER 8

old, but clean shower curtain hangs over the small square shower. A stack of neatly folded towels sits on a primitive wood shelf.

It's got the bare minimum, like most safe houses do.

With longing, I stare at the shower. Heavens, it would feel soooo good right now.

But there's no way I can take the chance of getting my wound wet. Scotch would kill me if I got the bandage soaked.

Or... maybe he'd spank me.

I grin, feeling sheepish. Lord, I must be intoxicated if I thought that!

Oh, I'm not averse to flirting. I like to flirt. But rule number one of the game is know who NOT to flirt with. And Jameson Scott, M.D. falls squarely in that category.

But what did I do? I flirted with the intent of provocation in the car, even though he's the kind of man that can take an innocent enough flirty comment and turn it into a fiasco.

*Yep*. Fiasco of almost six and a half foot proportions.

That's what getting involved with a man like him would be.

Hell. That's what getting involved with ninety-nine percent of men is. Which is why I steer clear and stay in my own lane.

But damn if he isn't doing a fine job of rattling me all to hell.

I lick across my lips, gliding my tongue across the place where I can still feel his mouth against mine.

I'm still pissed at myself for liking it.

But god, all I want is to feel alive. Really alive after facing down death. And what better way to feel that than in the arms of the one man who makes your blood sizzle?

Oh no!

I cringe. God, am I really going to let myself do something so reckless?

Maybe I do really have hero syndrome!

I wouldn't be the first person who got hearts in their eyes for the person who rescued them.

And that's a whole other set of problems that I don't want.

But first things first. Get clean. Get dressed. Get the heck out of San Miguel. Before I do something truly problematic.

When I look more closely in the mirror, I almost scream. *Mother of God.* Who is that looking back at me?

Frazzled hair, sunken eyes. Pale skin. I've aged ten years since Pavel pulled that trigger.

I don't need to worry too much about Scotch flirting with me or getting any ideas because I am a walking nightmare.

Looking at the sickly waif in the mirror makes me tired. So tired. Melted-bones-and-no-gas tired.

I lower myself onto the toilet and lean on the sink. The water that comes out of the spigot is tepid and vaguely the color of rust. But there is water, at least.

I almost forgot what third world countries are like. Laying low in the U.S. has made me soft. Or spoiled. I'm not sure which.

Dipping a washcloth in the sink, I clean myself slowly, from fingertips to toes, knocking off the dust and sweat. Working around the sling Scotch tied around my neck.

God, it feels good to scrub the grime away. Seeing all the mess reminds me how livid I am at Pavel. That slimy bastard.

Peering down at my bandage, the one carefully applied

by Scotch, I wonder why Pavel didn't take the chance to blow my head clean off.

I know that's what I'd have done to him if he hadn't had that poor child over his shoulder. It was too risky, even though I trust my aim.

But next time I see him, he's going to meet the business end of my new Sig Sauer. Because I am going to have a new one. Pronto.

And I won't miss... unless it's just to toy with him.

That idea amuses me enough to make me laugh out loud.

I finger-comb the tangles out of my hair with my one good arm and give myself a final onceover.

Not good.

But better. And now I only smell like swamp medicine and cheap soap. Shoving the hospital gown in the trash, I weave my way back into the bedroom. Acutely aware of the fact that I have none of my own clothing.

My well-worn boots. My... everything is gone. Except, apparently, my current disposable cell phone which Scotch rescued from my cargo pants.

I lean on the dresser, swaying a little as I pull open the drawers. The first two are empty. I squint into the third drawer, trying to understand what I'm seeing.

Okay, this is weird with a capital W.

A man's pair of boxers with rainbow stripes—

One hot pink string bikini set.

And a black leather bustier.

Oh, then there's the socks. A pair of tall white athletic socks with bright green bands around the top.

What the hell?

Great, this is just what I need. If only I was going to a rave. Or the beach in Brazil.

*Argh!*

I glance over my shoulder at the bathroom where the hospital gown is shoved into the top of the trash can. *No.* I'm not getting it out.

So, the immediate issue remains. I'm naked.

With two men in the house.

I hold up the bikini... hm. It's teeny. The triangles on the top aren't much bigger than pasties.

And the bustier... it might work. But I'd have to wear it with either the men's boxers or the thong bikini bottom. Great.

If only the boxers weren't ten sizes too big, they would be the sound choice. But without a belt, that's not happening.

I'll just demand Scotch or Andre give me one of their shirts for now and then someone's going to shop for me. I can't exactly leave to fly home dressed like a party favor.

I'm scowling at the nutty assortment of clothing options when the door to the bedroom pops open.

Oops.

Damn. Just what I need. More rattling of my thin control.

Scotch is frozen in the doorway staring at me... A look of disbelief on his rugged, handsome face.

I have no idea what to cover. But I know one thing. I don't have enough hands.

A little devil on my shoulder tells me that maybe I should cover nothing at all. "Uh, hi there."

Scotch steps inside the room. He kicks the door closed with the heel of his boot.

My pulse tears off at a sprint. "I got cleaned up and... I thought I'd put something else on."

"That looks like having nothing on instead of something."

I half roll my eyes and pfft. "He's got a flair for the obvious." I hold up the string bikini. "This is all that I found. You're going to have to get me some clothing since you cut mine off of me."

He steps toward me. "Fair enough." But he doesn't take his eyes off of me.

I feel that burning look to my bones. Deep in my marrow, where a powerful thirst for life lives. I want nothing more than to feel. Alive. Viciously alive right now.

And that somehow translates into a thirst for this man like I've never felt before.

His throat works as he swallows. "The bikini works."

And I flush warm from the tips of my toes to the top of my ears, and probably as pink as a flamingo.

Slowly, his eyes skim down my body, landing on all the places where my pulse is pounding.

"You've seen me naked already."

Scotch's voice is thick and deliciously sexy as it vibrates between us. "*That* was different."

I'm frozen, locked in his smoldering laser focus.

If I took a step, I know I'd fall.

Probably on my knees, right in front of his ginormous package. Where I'd promptly beg for something I really want, but shouldn't.

I swear I see his nostrils flare as if he's scenting me. "Damn if you aren't beautiful."

Left stammering, I falter as my ovaries take the helm. If there was any logic left in my brain, it's been overridden by a surge of pure iridescent hormones. "Thank you. But you don't have to lie. I saw myself in the mirror. Unless, of course, you have a thing for zombies."

His laughs would have to be sexy too. "The things that come out of your mouth never cease to surprise me."

"Like?"

"You propositioned me in the car."

I can't believe we're having this conversation with me standing bare naked in front of him. "I was high. What is that stuff, anyway?"

"A pain reliever. And aphrodisiac for some, according to the medicine man."

I squeeze my eyes shut. "Well, I guess it worked." But if I'm honest with myself I was hot for the man from the first minute I saw him that day he treated me in the emergency clinic. Even if he made me furious. My body was humming with lust, even though I instantly loathed him and his bossy, hulking attitude.

"You're still feeling the effects now?"

"I am. Less, but I'm still..."

Hot. So hot inside. I'm feeling too much. All of it. And the drug isn't half of it. What I'm feeling started long before the slimy aphrodisiac pain medicine got rubbed on me by the hottest doctor in the world.

How cruel is that? The first man that's even so much as heated my hooha up in years and it has to be him. The tall, chiseled, scalpel-wielding, protective man who threatens my foundation like a 9 on the Richter Scale.

He tips his chin. "Does the offer still stand?"

"For?"

"Kissing you again."

A little choked rumble vibrates my throat. "Now who's being forward?"

"I think we both are."

My mouth drops open. Holy smokes. "Did you use the medicine?"

## CHAPTER 8

He laughs before his voice drops low. "No. None needed."

Cool air stirs my skin. A sudden reminder that I'm standing here, naked except for my sling, having a conversation that I feel less and less control of.

I cross my one arm over my breasts.

His voice is so husky. So sexy. "Don't cover yourself. I want to look at you."

The air crackles between us as my pulse throbs between my legs. His eyes slide right down there...

The steady rise and fall of his chest increases. The air in the room heats up by a solid ten degrees.

Dropping my arm slowly back down to my side, I watch his expression turn hungrier.

I had no idea that eyes could convey pure carnal need with such force.

He takes another step toward me. Big and strong and one hundred percent virile male. When he speaks, the pitch of his rough, masculine words makes cells deep inside my body sing. "I told Andre I wasn't going to fuck you."

That makes me laugh hard enough that my nipples bounce. "You did?"

He nods once, "I'm pretty sure I lied."

Oh lord. The man is dark, delicious trouble. I shiver as the air stirs around my bare skin. He reaches for me slowly. "May I?"

Breathless, I nod. Apparently, my sensibility isn't the only thing Scotch steals.

I've felt the man's hands a dozen times before. Yet, this is *sooo* different. Like he's letting himself really touch me.

Never before has a jolt of heat shot from his fingertips straight to my womb. I fight the urge to press my legs together as a shiver races up my spine.

Gently, he traces the tip of his broad rough finger over the mound of my breast. The skin tingles beneath the pressure. His voice drops husky and low. "I'm about to break all the rules."

"Something tells me you've never been one to follow them."

"What gives you that idea?" He slowly glides that finger around my nipple, carefully avoiding the most sensitive bud.

I shrug my good shoulder. "A hunch. Like seeing like."

A long, slow breath passes between his lips as his eyes rise to mine. Deep brown pools of pure heat that swallow me whole. "I want you."

Before I even think, I'm proving my insanity and my need to take back my hold on feeling alive. "Then take me." I grab a fistful of his shirt.

He sucks in a breath through his nose. "Careful, beautiful. I'm unlike any loaded weapon you've handled."

Leaning into his hand, I murmur, "I'm not afraid of you."

With his other hand, he fists the back of his t-shirt and jerks it off over his head.

*Oh. My.*

A reckless smile bursts from me. Wherever they made the man, they did it right. Broad, ripped, and powerful. Sun kissed and smooth–he's a sight to behold.

And the abs... let's just say his six pack didn't come from the beer aisle.

*Mamma Mia.*

I want to trace every contour, feel every thick rope of muscle.

With my fingers.

With my tongue.

With my clit as he slides his body up mine.

As Scotch steps closer, a wave of heat comes off his big body and wraps me up.

His chest rumbles in warning. "You should be afraid."

My eyes drift closed as I savor the amazing feel of his hand moving with slow reverence against my heated skin. "Because?"

"Because I've never wanted a woman like I want you."

My eyes blink open. What I see stops my heart. He's freaking serious. Inside my chest, there's an instant arrhythmia.

"Liar," I say in jest because I don't want to hear that.

I don't want to be that to him. This is nothing more than two people satisfying a carnal urge.

His left hand slides around behind me, where he presses it's giant width across my low back. "I might be a lot of things. But if there's one thing I'm not, it's a liar."

I reach for him again and twist my fingers into the waist of his pants. "What are you, then?"

"Obsessed with you."

A deep want, greedy and hot, begins to unfurl in my belly. "That turns me on."

"It shouldn't. It should frighten the hell out of you. But again, you aren't the woman who blanches in the face of danger."

"No. I'm not."

I pull him toward me. As his mouth lowers to mine, I'm filled with his earthy, masculine scent. It drives fire into my blood.

But he stops, just an inch from me. His dark eyes look right into mine and make me weak from head to toe. "Are you sure you're sober enough to consent to this?"

I blink. "God. If that didn't sound like a doctor."

"The medicine lowers your inhibitions."

I wrap my hand around his neck and pull him down to nibble on that delicious bottom lip of his. "I'm high. I'm not out of my head. It's a little like taking molly."

His stormy brown eyes grow darker. "What do you know about taking molly?"

"Enough. I've seen and done a lot of things."

"I'm not sure I like hearing that."

"I'm not a slut if that's what you're worried about. I haven't been with a man in years."

He's silent and snapping with energy as my heart races behind my breastbone. The pads of his fingers flex against my back and my breast. "Am I a bastard for saying that makes me happy as hell?"

"I don't know. You tell me."

When he shoves his hand into my hair, I know I've won him over, and I've done what I said I'd never do—hook up with a doctor.

Damn him. Damn me.

Damn Pavel for shooting me. Because I'm breaking my own rules too. And enjoying it far too much.

Scotch's mouth collides with mine in a breathtakingly ravenous kiss.

This time, he's going for broke.

And I'm about to cash in.

And god, what a kiss. The man owns me as he turns my head for a deeper angle. My fingers dig into his lat as he steals my breath and makes my heart flip cartwheels.

His right hand cups my butt demandingly, and he lifts me clear off the floor. I can't hold back my throaty laugh. God, he's big. And strong. And hot as the sun itself.

When he sits onto the edge of the bed, I'm wrapped

around his waist. "Tell me if anything hurts," he says as he opens his mouth along the cord of my neck.

"Mmmm... hm. That doesn't hurt."

If he's going for broke, so am I. Because feeling alive never felt so good.

## CHAPTER NINE

*Scotch*

Walking in on Simona naked was the last thing in the world I needed to do. The situation couldn't be much worse.

Let me take that back. It could be a hell of a lot worse. Which is why maybe I feel like going after what I want.

Simona could have died on that operating table. Or in the back of that car. She could have bled out or coded or... hell, a hundred different things could have happened.

And I would have never gotten the chance to tell her she's fucking gorgeous. Or that her bristly attitude somehow turns me into a walking erection.

Or that I want to know her story.

Her favorite color.

The ice cream she always picks.

And the way she likes to be touched.

So, walking in on her, standing there, with the pale light

## CHAPTER 9

from the lamp painting her in pinks and golds, was the moment that I knew I had to have her.

Right here in San Miguel.

Right here in the safe house.

While Andre guards us. Because yes, I'm a greedy fucker. And life is short.

Too fucking short.

And everything about the last few hours proved that once again.

I should be saying 'hell, no'.

Instead, I'm trying to figure out how I can get my hungry cock deep inside her tight curvy body without busting her wounds up.

It's wrong. And I know it, but when she wraps those slender sexy fingers around me, I do nothing but shudder. "We have to be careful. You're injured..."

"You can fix me. You've already proven that."

I laugh at her. At the insanity of the moment. "You're crazy."

"Only a little." She smiles and chuckles darkly. "Okay, maybe a lot."

I lean up and kiss her. Slowly and gently. Because if I don't slow down, the animal in me is going to gain control of the situation. And I'll give in to the dangerous urge to flip her under me and claim her with vicious, pounding thrusts.

Slow is better. And just as I wanted, she melts into me, still and soft, as her delicate hand circles my throbbing erection.

This tender, quiet Simona is far from the snappy, glaring woman who sat across the seat from me a few hours ago. I'm not sure which I like better. Or maybe I love them both.

Kissing along her silky-smooth cheek, then pressing my

mouth against her neck, I inhale the scent that's been driving me wild since I got on the plane with her in Utah.

While everyone else rambled and ranted about this and that, my mind was wandering down roads that all headed to one place. Her tight heat wrapped around me.

I just didn't picture it like this.

Hell, I thought it would be more of a battle to win her over.

More chase. More convincing her that I'm not the devil.

But I'm happy as hell that I have the chance right now to explore the delicate curve of her ear with my mouth. "You can hate me another time. Right now, let's forget whatever hang-up you have with doctors and men."

She smiles against my lips. "I have a feeling I'm going to like your manhood."

"That's my intent."

Touching her feels so damned good. It burns away all the ugliness in the world. Skin like perfect velvet covers her narrow waist. I glide my hand to her hip, then trace down the fold of her thigh to the vee between her legs.

Simona murmurs something in a language I don't know, as I brush my fingers over her hot, wet labia. "So juicy. Like a perfect peach."

She shivers at my touch as her eyes drift closed. Oh, yes indeed. I like her like this.

"There's a condom in my wallet. Thanks to some patron saint of sex looking out for us."

"That's good, but I've got an implant, so we could...."

"I know about the implant."

Her pale blue eyes refocus on mine. "How?"

"I felt it in your arm."

"You really did look me over..."

## CHAPTER 9

"I did, but I haven't seen this mysterious tattoo on your labia..."

She giggles and I slide her off of my lap and drop to my knees on the floor in front of her incredible body. I nip at her belly as I smooth over a lingering tan line. And below that, my focus lands on her clean-shaved, mouthwateringly sexy pussy. "I think I should have a look. With my tongue."

That shocks a little gasp out of her. "God, you're so dirty—" But her words vanish when I swipe my tongue over her clit and swirl it around that tiny bundle of nerves.

The fingers of her free hand, the one that's not bound in the sling, curl into my short-cropped hair.

With the back of my hand, I lift her thigh until her knee is resting on the bed. "Just like that, open for me, my sexy Sprite."

She growls my name. "Scotch..."

With a few deep thrusts of my tongue in just the right spot, I quickly make her forget any complaint about me using the nickname the team gave her.

The next time she speaks, it's to tell me how good my mouth feels on her. She moans as her short nails dig into my scalp. "Oh, I could come like that."

"How about like this?" I slip a finger, then a second into her wet heat and curl against her g-spot.

"Scotch. *Scotch!*" she whispers hoarsely, "I might scream."

I laugh. "You didn't need to tell me that you were a screamer. I knew that already."

She twists against me as she soaks my hand.

"Don't make me embarrass us."

"Honey, nothing you can do will embarrass me. Fuck. I mean, every man loves making a woman scream when she comes."

"Andre—"

"He knows the deal."

I rise to stand in front of her, pulling her against me, pressing my steel-hard erection against her stomach, all while keeping my fingers buried in her deliciously wet core. "I've got the antidote. Scream away."

Our mouths crash together. Thrusting my tongue, I match the rhythm of my fingers. Hungrily devouring the delicious sweetness between her parted lips.

Her tongue dances with mine, she rides my hand, as I push her recklessly toward climax. I nearly lose my ever-loving mind. This is madness.

I shouldn't want her. But want is long since gone. Hell, I need her.

And I have no idea how I'm going to fit inside her sweet little pussy because she's so tight. But damn if I'm not going to try.

Simona's slender back suddenly stiffens. A powerful wave of contractions clench around my fingers. I press harder against her g-spot, as I drive my tongue and fingers deeper into her.

A song of whimpers rises from her throat. And every one of them turns up the heat. Ratchets my blood to a boiling, dangerous cocktail of testosterone and possessiveness.

Fuck. Yes.

Then she comes.

And like everything about Simona, it's explosive.

Oh, she is a screamer. But I capture it and swallow it down.

Wrapping my arm tightly around her waist, I stop her from bucking herself totally out of my grip.

She pants against me as her body trembles from the

# CHAPTER 9

intense climax. The hair along her temple is damp when I press my lips there. "That was hot as hell, firecracker."

She laughs, hoarsely. "Did you learn that in medical school?"

"Not in class."

Rubbing my hand over her hair, I lean down to meet her eyes. "I didn't hurt you, did I?"

"Lord, no. Do I look like I'm in pain? That was unreal."

I catch her lips with mine again. Her kiss is hungry, but I slow us down. When I pull back, I say five words that hurt like my hand is being crushed in a vice. "I think we should stop."

Her eyes fly wide. "What? Are you crazy?"

"Obviously, but I think it would be best. Another time..."

She looks past my shoulder to the dresser where my pistol's sitting. "Prepare to lose body parts."

I shake my head. Jesus. I want her. But I'm too big. I'll be too rough. Somehow, I manage to say, "Babe, you need to rest before we have to bust out of here and scramble to the airport."

"Listen here. You're already on thin ice. If you leave me hanging like this, we've got a serious problem. A capital offense."

Groaning, I try to pull back, but she catches my cock in her warm, strong fingers. "Oh no, you don't."

"Simona. This is dangerous. Do you have any idea how I want to fuck you right now?"

She shrugs her good shoulder and a devilish smile curls her lips. "With your penis, I presume."

Clenching my teeth, I think of a dozen reasons why I should stop this, and one reason why I shouldn't. Because I *want* her.

This might be it for us. One night. One chance to taste something that draws me like a moth to flame.

I snarl as my body shakes with pure animal energy. "I want to bend you over that bed. I want to sink myself so deep inside of that crazy tight pussy of yours that you will feel me for a week."

She swallows roughly. And blinks up at me as she licks lips that are reddened from my kiss.

Her voice is totally breathy. "Um. That's seriously hot, Dr. Scott."

I drop my forehead against hers as I fight the fevered rate of my breathing. "I want to fold you up beneath me." Pressing my mouth against her ear, I let my hunger show in my voice. "Lock your knees up by your shoulders with my chest. And pound that hot little body of yours until I can't pump anymore."

Her skin heats beneath my mouth. The rate of her breathing accelerates as she strokes my cock from base to tip, milking a growl from me. My chest is filled with fire as I say, "I want to smash you against that wall and fuck you till we're both raw and broken, and you scream my name until the rafters shake."

The pulse in her neck pounds wildly. Her tongue traces across those lips again. "You are not what I expected."

Gripping her hand, where she's got it wrapped around me, I remind her, "I warned you. So, you can see why we need to stop right now."

"No. I don't agree. I'm not broken. I can take it."

Anger flares in my gut. "Look—"

She presses her finger to my lips. "Scotch. Shut up. Now I'm going to walk over to that wall and you're going to get behind me, and you're going to give me a good fucking end to a really bad day."

## CHAPTER 9

I'm stunned silent as she steps back and turns her beautiful ass toward me. When she gets to the wall, she braces her good hand, and spreads her legs. For me.

Closing my eyes, I curse. A loud, long stream of filthy words. "What the hell have you done to me?"

"Nothing yet. But I have plans."

As I stalk toward her, my jutting cock is fisted in my hand. "I bet you do."

I know I've lost my mind when I bite her neck and shove myself into her bare.

## CHAPTER TEN

# Simona

Scotch's powerful body drives into me in one hard stroke.

Woman down. I'm done. Lost at sea, as he claims me with a second hard stroke.

I bite down hard on my lip to stop the cry of pleasure that threatens to rip from my throat. God. It hurts. So good.

Deliciously stretching me, filling me like I've never been filled before.

Planting his hand above my hand, Scotch holds me against his body so I don't have to brace myself. Then he thrusts into me over and over again until I'm panting. Moaning. Worshiping him with my throaty cries.

When I don't think I can take any more, he shifts and angles deeper. Groaning, I drop my head and shudder. I know I'm going to scream. Nothing's going to stop me. Fire is building in my veins and has to have a release.

"I swear, my little Sprite, you're so hot and tight.

# CHAPTER 10

Choking my cock. I'm not going to last long. But I promise, next time, I'll keep you up all night long."

I pant, trying to catch my breath. "I'm close—"

"Come for me, beautiful. Come hard." His arm tightens around me, pulling me harder back against his thrusts. My world starts to dim. Only the place where he's deep inside of me is in focus. My whole being narrows down to those few inches of space.

It's so good. So beautiful. So powerful. The pleasure so all-consuming that tears leak from my eyes. "Scotch. Oh, yessss!"

Growling like a wild animal, he thrusts fast and hard and drives right through my release. I don't even have time to form a scream, I'm so engulfed in ecstasy that my vision blinks black.

His slick chest presses against my back. His heat surrounds me, shattering my heart into a million fragments of light.

Through gritted teeth, he mutters, "Oh, Simona, fuck. Yes!"

I'm weak with pleasure when he lowers us down to the floor, pulling me down to sit on his folded thighs. His breath is rough against my neck, his heart pounding against my back as we both fight to get our control.

When he starts laughing, it surprises me.

"Holy hell, woman. Your tight little kitten nearly choked my dick to death."

I can't even think of a reply or contain the laughter that starts somewhere in my womb.

When I catch my breath, I say, "Well, if your goal was for me to feel you for a week, then I think you've succeeded. How big is that thing, anyway?"

He laughs softly against my shoulder. "Enough." He

wraps me in his arms, cocooning me in his strength. "We're both officially certifiable."

"I guess that's better than one of us."

He cups my lower tummy with his hand, then slides his fingers down between my swollen folds where our bodies are still joined. "You did it. How could I resist this? When I walked in on you naked, I knew it was useless to fight my urges anymore. You won."

A sound comes from the living room. He groans. "I need to get up. We might have to move out soon, and you're definitely not wearing that bikini. At least for anyone else to see."

When I rise up, letting him slide out, his milky semen coats my thigh. It's one of those things that startles you even though it shouldn't.

I was fully aware he wasn't covered. But only twice have I had sex without a condom. My first time, and this. For some reason, I wanted Scotch skin to skin with me. No barriers. No pretenses.

He sees where I'm looking and traces his finger through the moisture. "Fuck if that isn't sexy, seeing my seed all over you."

I'm breathless, frozen for a few seconds as my heart pounds. "I... I should get cleaned up."

Scotch stands, offers his hand. "Let me help you."

I let him pull me up. "I'm okay. I'd prefer to, you know, clean up on my own."

His dark brown eyes are serious as he stares down at me. "Of course. I'm going to leave to get some clothing and food for you."

I reach for the wall and half stumble toward the bathroom. I hold up a hand when he reaches for me. "I'm fine. I just had to get my balance. I promise."

With a clenched jaw, he watches me. "Andre's here. Just yell for him if you need anything. I mean anything."

I nod and close myself into the bathroom where I can try to get my head back on straight in private.

Because lord knows, I'm not in any place to face the man. The clock is ticking down fast to meltdown mode.

## CHAPTER ELEVEN

*Scotch*

Watching Simona close that bathroom door is about as rough as getting kicked in the gut.

Damnit. I know we were running hot and the cliff of disaster was too close for comfort.

I raise a hand to knock, then stop myself. I shove my junk back in my tactical pants, zip up, and raise my hand again. Instead, I just reach for the knob. "I'm coming in."

"Don't."

"Talk to me."

The silence on the other side of the door is deafening. I turn the knob.

The sight inside makes my heart crease into a wad like wrinkled newspaper. Simona's gripping the sink, staring at her reflection.

"Hey." I reach for her. She shies away.

While I respect her totally, I'm not letting her have an emotional crash on her own. "Come here." I wrap my arms around her. "No regrets. Okay?"

She shakes her head a little, sighs. "I'm a mess. I wanted that, what we did, but now I don't have a clue what I'm feeling."

Looking at our reflections in the mirror, I admit, "Neither do I."

"We shouldn't have—"

"No regrets. It was amazing. And you know what? I feel alive and damn grateful to be standing here feeling things in my head and heart that only a very alive person feels."

She closes her eyes and drops her head. "I do feel alive. And I owe you for that."

I tilt her chin up so I can see her eyes in the mirror. "Is that why you gave yourself to me? Because you felt a debt?"

"I don't know. Maybe part of it."

"That wasn't what this was about for me."

Her frown deepens and a little line forms between her brows. "No. I wanted you."

"I hear a 'but' in there."

She licks her lips as her eyes drift away. "I've never owed anyone for my life before."

"You don't owe me."

Breathless, she says, "Yes, I do."

"Buy me dinner."

Her mouth drops open, then snaps closed. "That was random."

"No, seriously, buy me dinner and you can call it even, if that feels better to you." Of course, my motive is to get her to dinner as well. Any minute I can steal with her, I'll take.

She groans, "Scotch. You're ridiculous. I'm sorry. I just

need to be alone right now. Okay? There's just so much going on. I feel exhausted."

Brushing her hair aside, I ask, "I understand. How can I help?"

"Food. Clothes. Keeping me safe."

I hold her tight for a few seconds more with my brain sending me all kinds of mixed-up signals. "I'll be back as soon as I can."

She watches me in the mirror as I step back. "Scotch. Be careful out there."

"I will."

Andre's sitting by the window, gun in his arms when I close the bedroom door. "I'm going out for some things."

"Are you sure?"

"We need some food, and I need to get some clothing for her."

"Make it brief, friend. This place is sketchy as fuck."

"You don't have to tell me. I could hear people yelling and gunshots."

His scowl turns darker. "I'll be a lot happier when we're on that plane."

"That makes three of us. Hey, listen out for her. She's up, but I'm worried about her."

He watches me, something unsaid in his expression.

As I reach for the door, he says, "You didn't fuck with her head, did you?"

"No worse than she fucked with mine."

He watches me for a minute, then nods once.

"Use her nickname as the codeword when you get back."

"Copy."

When I slip out the door, I have a feeling he's not too

# CHAPTER 11

happy with me, which makes me wonder what his real feelings for Simona are.

* * *

DUCKING INTO THE ALLEY, I wait for a group of young guys with guns to hustle by. When they are long past, I turn the last corner in the narrow alley, and climb the stairs to the safe house apartment.

I knock once and murmur the codeword. The latch clicks. It takes a few seconds for Andre to open the three chains.

"Some empanadas in there for you." I set the bag on the table. "She come out?"

"No. Not a sound since you left."

My gut is twitchy when I walk to the door. I force a breath when I knock, "Hey, got food and clothes."

"Come in."

I slip inside the door. Simona's propped up in bed with the thin cotton blanket tucked around her.

"How are you feeling?"

"Better."

I hold up two bags. "Food. Clothes. Which would you like first?"

She smiles, almost shyly. "Food."

"Good choice." I move to the side of the bed. She slides over, so I sit on the edge. "Potato and beef empanadas."

"They smell delicious."

I pass her a bottle of water. "They are, I cheated and had one while they packed up the order."

She picks up an empanada. "I don't blame you. I wouldn't have waited either."

Her eyes drift closed as she chews the first bite. "Oh god. So good. I didn't realize I was starving."

Watching her makes my body edgy as hell. She's not the only one that's starved. But for a whole different thing.

"The city's getting pretty stirred up. We're hoping to get out of here soon. As soon as you eat, you should dress."

We share the rest of the food in silence for a while.

Simona smiles fondly. "I remember the first time I had empanadas. God, they were so good, I ate until I could barely move."

"Was that where you grew up?"

"No, I spent my early life in Czech. The land of soups and stews."

"And your more recent life?"

"All over."

"I heard you worked in intelligence."

She visibly shuts down. "So to speak. How about you, where did you live?"

I chew the bite of empanada I just shoved in my mouth as I hold up a finger while I swallow. "Navy brat. I've lived everywhere."

That seems to ease her a bit. "Guess we have that in common."

"Do you ever go home?"

She glances down, picks up the last little pieces of empanada off of the paper plate. "I haven't in a long time. I didn't think it was safe."

That makes my skin bristle. "Has this man, Pavel, been hunting you?"

"No. He hasn't been on my radar in years. Until today—"

Andre knocks on the door. "We've got to roll. Now."

Simona kicks her feet to the side of the bed. I swipe up

# CHAPTER 11

the food wrappers. "Let's get you dressed. We'll be right out, man."

When he's out of ear shot, I say, "He's protective of you."

"All the Agile guys act like brothers."

"That's a good thing."

She grumbles, "Sometimes."

The button-up shirt easily goes over her shoulder. She watches my fingers work as I fasten it up over her bare breasts. "Sorry, no bras. Luckily, I found a shirt with buttons."

I have to count to a thousand while I shimmy a pair of tights up her long, sexy legs.

She seems almost shy, so I keep my comments to myself.

"We can apply more of the medication in the plane once we take off."

Her cheeks turn pink. "Are you sure that's a good idea?"

It's my turn to grin. "I seem to remember someone mentioning the mile high club."

She swats me. "Go. Get out of here."

## CHAPTER TWELVE

## Simona

San Miguel has the worst roads in the world. "Can they have any more pot holes? Is that possible?"

Andre glances in the mirrors again, checking all the angles. "You obviously haven't been to downtown Newark."

Scotch laughs even though his eyes are serious as he scans the road around us. "You might be right."

Andre hurtles us toward the small airport on the outskirts of the city as the thickest part of night settles in. The streets are still wild with people carrying guns, but no one bothers us as Andre falls in with other speeding cars.

"Thank god," I mutter when I finally see the blinking runway lights. "Have they touched down?"

"Not yet, they're waiting on word from us that we're pulling in."

Scotch cues up the satellite phone. "We're two minutes

from the parking area." He listens for a few seconds. "Roger. See you then."

"South end. This is going to be a dash." He turns, his expression gravely worried. "Can you handle running?"

"Uh. I'm not sure."

"I think I should carry you."

Gritting my teeth, I admit maybe that is the best idea. "I'm still feeling kind of weak."

"You lost a lot of blood."

We bump over the broken entrance to the airport. I grimace. "How much did I lose exactly?"

"Enough for a transfusion," comments Andre.

I'm sure my face must register my shock. Scotch says, "It's not uncommon in a situation like yours."

"So, I have someone else's blood in my veins?"

Andre glances up in the review mirror, then at Scotch.

"Yes, mine, technically," Scotch says as we come to a screeching halt on the paved lot next to the runway.

"Yours?" I half screech.

He's dragging me from the car and swinging me up in his big arms before I can protest. I can only grit and grimace as he runs. All the jolting freaking hurts like hell.

The air stairs drop down from the jet with a whoosh. Lit by low interior light, Marshall's profile fills the doorway.

"Holy cow, Sprite, you scared the life out of me."

"Me too!" echoes Sierra from the pilot's seat. "Now hurry up, boys. We're wheels up in two minutes."

The guys hustle us inside. Scotch eases me into a chair and buckles me in.

I grab his arm. "We've got something to talk about, don't go anywhere."

"I'm not." He folds his big frame into the seat next to me

and buckles up. "We're set. Ready for takeoff," he calls to Sierra.

Marshall and Andre take their places as the engines begin to roar. In just a few seconds, we're tearing down the runway.

Pain throbs in my shoulder. I'm wiped out. All I can do is sit back as we take flight into the night sky.

Turning my face to the window, I watch the lights of Selva Oscura becoming smaller and smaller below. I'll never forget the place. And not just because I nearly lost my life there. Because I gave up part of my sanity, and maybe even a little part of my heart there too.

I won't be forgetting the intense heat I shared with the man next to me until the day I die.

Once we're at a steady cruising altitude, Scotch unbuckles and disappears into the back of the plane.

The scent of soap surrounds him when he returns. Good, strong soap. And I know he's washed his hands because he's going to work on my wound.

He unloads his pockets, sitting the medical supplies on the small table next to us. "Let's get some pain medication on you."

I watch as he unbuttons my shirt, pushes my sling aside and exposes my wound from below the bandage.

With care, he applies more of the muddy-looking gunk using the special wooden stick the medical man provided. A clean bandage is applied. The sling fitted once again.

As the pain starts to ease, I finally feel like talking. "You gave me your blood?"

"I did."

"What does that mean to you?"

His eyes lift to mine. "It means I gave you my blood."

"How do you feel about knowing your lifeblood is circulating in my body?"

He seems to consider that for a few minutes as he puts the supplies back into his pockets. "It feels like service. Part of what I am committed to as a doctor."

"I can't imagine what that's like."

"You've never given blood?"

I shake my head. "No. I've never really thought about it."

"It's a really powerful gift to give."

"You don't have to tell me."

He leans back in the seat, turns his head toward me. "How do you feel about it? About having part of me inside of your veins?"

I let my eyes drift closed for a second as I feel the warmth inside of my body. "Grateful, first." I take a long, slow breath, soaking in the relief of being safe, on the plane, on my way home. Alive. "And, somehow, it feels intimate. Which is kind of crazy, I know." I laugh lightly. "I'm sure you've given blood to others. Even other soldiers, so I know what I'm saying sounds nutty."

Scotch catches the hand I've been waving around as I talk, he pulls it across until it's caught against his chest, right over his heart. "Knowing it is there, in you, feels different for me too."

I stare at him as my heart rages and tries to escape. "You can't be getting the feels for me, Doctor. I'm not the catching type."

We're locked, staring at each other for a long, long minute. Then he laughs. "I've always felt the same about myself. I'm not relationship material."

"Well, that's another thing we have in common. On top

of the fact that we both like empanadas. We both lived all over. *And* we both share the same blood, now."

He swallows roughly and lets some kind of deeper emotion show on his face. My insides warm up even more and my heart feels like it grows behind my ribcage.

I'd like to blame it on the medication, but somehow, I worry this is far deeper than a buzz.

Which is a lot harder to solve than washing some salve off.

The hiss of the air purification system and jet engines surrounds us. And I can't pull my eyes away. His heart beats steadily but hard below my palm. "What's going on in there?"

"Something I'm not familiar with."

We sit like that for far too long, as turbulence bumps the jet around, with me feeling that strong pulse, knowing the rhythm of my own has decided to pace along.

He pushes a stray lock of my hair back behind my ear. "Where will you spend your recovery?"

Tension unfurls in my belly. This is what I was thinking about while he was gone earlier. "I don't know. If Pavel saw me, I have a strange feeling he's going to be hunting for me. Something just doesn't add up. And I've learned a long time ago to trust that instinct. I think it's a bad idea to go back to my place. Not that it was really much of a place. Just a cheap rented studio. My belongings could fit in a couple of duffel bags."

Quickly, Scotch speaks up. "I know of a place you can go."

Eyeing him suspiciously, I say, "No. I'm not coming to your place."

"While I'd enjoy the hell out of it, I wasn't suggesting it.

# CHAPTER 12

I know of an apartment, owned by a friend that no one else will know about."

"You think I could spend a couple weeks there?"

"I'm sure it would be fine. It's a rich friend that is out of the country. He never uses the place. I'll make some calls when we get closer."

"Scotch, why are you... you know. Being so nice to me?"

He blinks a few times as his brow creases. "Do you really need to ask?"

Embarrassed, I turn away, pulling my hand away from his chest. I can't admit that I don't trust anyone's motives. It's too hard to say out loud.

"Look, I know that you feel a bit untethered at the moment. Let me help out. No obligation for you to return the favor."

I let out a big breath. He leans in, close enough for just me to hear. "But I'm still holding you to that offer for dinner."

## CHAPTER THIRTEEN

*Scotch*

The small clock on the nightstand in Will's apartment says it's four am. Which day it is, I'm not so sure about. I'm spent. Flying for hours on end and driving from the airport was the icing on a hell of a cake of angst.

"Crawl in." I turn back the blanket for Simona.

She doesn't argue, which I know means she's as tired as I am.

I rub my hands over my gritty eyes, barely able to focus.

"You can't drive like that."

"I realize that. I'm going to crash on the couch."

She watches me warily as I pull the blanket up and lower it over her small body. "I'll change the dressing in a few hours. I'm not much good right now."

"I still can't believe you got us here. I have no clue how you drove with such little sleep."

"I wanted you to have a comfortable bed tonight. Well, this morning, technically."

"Thank you. I really appreciate that."

I rub my hand over her head, half checking her temperature, half just to touch her. "Rest up, Sprite. I'll be in to check on you in a few hours."

When I pull back, she grabs my hand. "Come, lie down."

"No, I'll take the couch."

"Don't be stupid. That couch looks like it's made of concrete."

I grin. "It is sort of weird looking. Weird modern shit."

She flips down the blanket again. "Get your ass in here."

"You don't have to worry about me taking advantage of you, I'm too tired."

"Come on. Just stop mansplaining and get in here."

I sag onto the side of the bed. She tugs me down. "Don't worry, I'm too tired to take advantage of you too."

"Well, aren't we quite the pair."

I extend my arm as I settle on the pillow and slip it under her neck. "No grumbling. I'm going to hold you." And imagine spending every night like this.

"Why?"

I close my eyes. "Because I'll know if you get up." And I want you in my arms, curled against me. So I can hear you breathing as you fall asleep and wonder about the dreams that fill your mind.

"Always the doctor."

"Yep, now go to sleep, Sprite."

She jabs a finger in my ribs, but soon softens against me.

When I drift off, I have a bittersweet feeling in my chest. The first woman who's really captured my attention in forever is lying along my side. If I was a betting man, I'd say the chances of this lasting are close to zero.

## CHAPTER FOURTEEN

## Simona

I'm rubbing the sleep from my eyes when I see the note on the kitchen counter. I must have been sleeping like the dead.

***Be back shortly. Take it easy. I'm picking up some of your things and provisions for the apartment.***

No signature. None needed.

Next to the neatly written note lies a Glock nine millimeter pistol. The one Scotch was carrying in San Miguel. A spare clip, fully loaded, lies next to it.

An appreciative warmth fills my chest. He knew I'd feel lost without my weapon.

Dr. Jameson Scott.

Man of many facets.

Protector extraordinaire.

Kindred spirit? The verdict is out.

I fill a glass of water at the sleek stainless sink and look out over the mountain landscape beyond the window. Feeling appreciative. Feeling... is that happiness in my chest?

Outside the window clouds moving over the terrain, casting shadows over the ridges and valleys. The mountains are different here than in Eden, even though I'm less than an hour away.

Today is a good day. My head feels clearer. My body less painful. Some of my energy has returned. And with it, my sense of curiosity and unease about the situation with Pavel.

Slowly, I walk through the apartment. It's clean, sleek, and obviously not lived in. A second home. Maybe a third. Maybe a ski destination hangout for Scotch's rich friend.

In each room, I stop at the window to inspect the surrounding terrain, familiarizing myself with possible escape routes. Looking for possible places for someone to hide.

After my rounds of the windows, I return to the kitchen to look for food and drink.

I've got my head in the fridge, staring at a small assortment of fizzy drinks and unopened condiments when it hits. A very familiar creeping sensation up the back of my neck.

One doesn't survive long in the spy business without acknowledging their sixth sense.

Shoving the pistol and spare clip in the back of my

tights, the only clothing I have on, I move silently to the long window at the end of the kitchen. Keeping myself out of sight, I inspect the terrain below.

It's ten feet to the ground. Evergreen shrubs and trees dot the carefully manicured property. Slowly, I scan the tree silhouettes for unusual shapes.

Finally, I take a breath. *Okay, you're just imagining things.*

But I can't shake the feeling. So, I go another round of all the windows.

Forty minutes have passed when I feel satisfied that nothing is amiss outside. At least, that I can see. So, I turn my attention to the interior of the apartment.

If only I had my electronic bug sniffer. But that's at my apartment. So, for now, I'll have to rely on good old-fashioned snooping.

Systematically, I look through the living room. Lifting the framed art, the decorative statues, the pillows, and coasters. Feeling moderately satisfied, I move to the bedroom.

Spinning in the center of the room, I take in all the places I'd hide a camera if it was me spying. There are at least twenty spots. One by one, I investigate. Not in the clock. Not in the mirror. Not in the—

*Oh no!* I gasp. Then curse. My fingers shake as I pick at the decorative emblem on the lamp. *My god.* Tucked in the corner of the gold emblem is a tiny camera. A very tiny, very expensive camera.

My stomach cinches tight. *No! This is not happening.*

Stumbling back, I fight to control my breathing.

Did Scotch know?

Would he do this?

Why would he bring me to an apartment that's bugged?

Or did somehow Pavel intercept the call about the

apartment last night when we were flying. No, that makes no sense. It was a satellite phone. One that Marshall feels secure using.

Nothing makes sense!

I'm fully hyperventilating when I realize I have nothing solid to go on. Nothing to make me believe that I'm safe. Nothing to support that Scotch is in on this. And the only thing to do in a situation like this—assume the worst.

Okay. Come on, Simona. Get your crap together. You know what to do. I force a diaphragmatic breath to calm my nervous system.

When I turn, that's when I catch sight of a second camera, over the doorway. Tiny, white, and barely visible. Invisible to the untrained eye.

My whole body feels disjointed as I stumble to the bathroom. I quickly gather all of the medical supplies into a spare trash bag, then I rush back to the bedroom. My button up shirt is laying on the chair, unbuttoned. I can't do it myself with the sling on, so I lift the sling over my head and toss it to the ground.

Growling, I shove my injured arm into the shirt sleeve. Jesus. It hurts like hell. My fingers fumble with the buttons. Of course I get them misaligned, off by one button. But that's the last thing I'm worried about.

Shoving my feet into the cheap plastic flip flops that Scotch bought along with the clothes, I fly toward the front door.

When I stand up on tiptoes to look out the peephole, I almost scream.

A man is right outside the door.

Bang! Bang! Bang!

Heart pounding so hard I can barely hold my body still,

## CHAPTER 14

I stare at the delivery man who's knocking on the door with a scowl on his face.

Wearing a nondescript blue uniform, the man has a plain brown box, the size of a brick in his gloved hand.

People wear gloves when they commit crimes. Heinous crimes.

Leveling my pistol on the door, I carefully back away.

*Fuck.*

Someone could have seen me on the cameras and known I was going to run. So, they sent in an operative.

My only option is the window in the hallway. It opens over a small covered porch for the apartment below.

The plastic bag is a total hindrance, I drop it on the floor and concentrate on getting myself through the window with only one arm. Nothing's easy like this.

The outside air is shockingly cold when I push myself out onto the roof. Scanning the terrain, I feel only mildly confident I can get to cover before someone could grab me or gun me down.

But I feel better on the run.

It's my natural inclination.

Always has been.

Always will be.

## CHAPTER FIFTEEN

*Scotch*

I'm twenty minutes from the apartment and feeling eager to see Simona when my cell phone rings.

"Scotch. Where are you?"

"Hey, Will, halfway between Eden and Park City. What's up?"

"Does your girl have a thing for running around half naked with a gun?"

"Fuck. Did you see something on a security camera?"

"Yeah. Something weird as hell."

I mash the accelerator on my Tahoe to the floor. "Spit it out."

"Someone knocked on the door, set off the camera on the outside, then the camera on the inside turned on. A blonde chic was pointing a pistol at the door."

# CHAPTER 15

"Son of a bitch!" I bellow in the phone. "What happened? Who was at the door? Did she open the door?"

"No, she didn't. The guy left after a few minutes. He was wearing a blue uniform that I didn't recognize, and... he had on gloves."

My heart jolts, then tries to choke me.

"God! Who wears fucking gloves when it's fifty degrees out?"

Will huffs and I know he's not telling me everything. "Scotch. She climbed out the window... I saw her on the building cam. I hacked into the complex security system a few months ago. So, I decided to check things out to see if anything else was up. That's when I saw her running across the lawn in a tactical stance, gun drawn."

I swerve around a slow ass Cadillac. "Dammit! I gotta go. Call me if you see anything else."

As soon as the call disconnects, I dial Simona. The line goes right to voicemail.

"Simona. Call me. I know you left the apartment. I'll help you. Call me!"

I furiously look in my contacts for Marshall. He answers on the first ring.

"Simona's on the run. Injured. Spooked by something."

"When?"

I relay the story. When I'm done, he sounds grim. "She's going to be hard to find."

"You don't have to tell me that. I already have a feel for her."

"Does she trust you?"

"I thought she did."

He sighs. "Does she have a way to reach you?"

"She's got my number. But she may reach out to you."

"Roger. I'll be in touch."

Something in his voice makes me unsure. "You know I'm one of the good guys, right?"

His breathing is steady on the other end. "You come highly regarded by people I trust."

"I don't know what's happening with her right now, but there's a lot of unanswered questions with the shooting. That worries the hell out of me. Does she have anyone she'd turn to?"

"Look, Simona's, shall we say, locked up tight as a vault. We met on a plane and somehow got into talking about spy craft. I was reading one of those fiction paperbacks for entertainment. I told her about my new company. She wanted some work. I hired her as a bodyguard. She's obviously a lot more than that. But not once has she told me a single personal thing about her life. I'll ask the team to see if anyone else has a clue. Sit tight. She might come back."

Feeling hot anger in my chest, I clench the steering wheel. "I can't see that happening."

"I'll send someone to watch her apartment."

"She's not going there."

Marshall holds his hand over his phone and says something to someone else. When he returns, he says, "I put eyes on the airports too."

"Thanks, man. Did you find out anything about Pavel?"

"He wasn't the original kidnapper, as you know. I think he was there to get the girl so he could ransom her for even more. He's got a reputation for doing whatever pays the most."

"Bastard."

"Yep, from everything I can see, you're right."

"Where's his home base?"

"Rumors say Paris."

## CHAPTER 15

"That's not good." Paris is one of those cities where you can disappear in the blink of an eye.

"She's going after him." Alone.

"Not yet," he says, "She's going to need to recover first."

"That's not going to take long." If she climbed out of a window and jumped off the roof, she's probably not too averse to chasing after fuckface.

Marshall says, "Maybe she lays low long enough for us to help."

"If we find them."

## CHAPTER SIXTEEN

# Simona

The clerk's smile is as plastic as the bag she hands me. I lift it with a muttered thanks and step out into the dark street as I shove the new burner phone in my pocket.

As I walk through the darkened park, I pull the phone out of the wrapper and power it up.

After four rings, the line clicks open. I say, "Moon over still waters."

A soft laugh comes over the line. My heart squeezes at the familiar sound.

"It's been a while, my child. I was starting to wonder."

The voice of Josef Novotny, my beloved rescuer, mentor, and friend, instantly soothes me.

"I'm sorry it's been so long, dear friend. How are you?"

"Old, crickety. Happy enough."

"I'm glad. Are you working?"

"Doing research for a book."

Which I know is code speak for him still working in intel. Maybe not in the field as much at the age of seventy, but still using his uncanny ability as a spy to fix the wrongs of the world.

"How about you? Enjoying being a nanny?"

"It was boring. I needed a break from the monotony."

He laughs. "So like you, I knew you'd be on the hunt for another job before long."

My insides tighten with a cold rush of dread. "Another job might have found me."

The line goes silent and I know he's reading between my words.

"Anyway, I just need to get some things together and enjoy some travel before I start this new opportunity."

He makes a *hmmm* sound. "I see."

"I'm thinking of visiting Sweden." Code speak for one of our drops.

"Sweden's nice this time of year. I heard the weather's going to be pleasant there tomorrow."

"I didn't realize it. I should look more carefully at the forecast." After a beat, I say, "I might want some travel advice."

He's smiling, I hear it on the other end. "Of course. Call me anytime, once you arrive there. I'll be sure to refresh my memory."

"I love you, my friend, stay warm and safe."

"Always, my dear. Be sure to get in touch right away once you reach Sweden."

"Of course. Goodbye."

Tears are standing on my lashes when I hang up. It's always hard to say goodbye to the only father figure I ever knew. The only person I've ever truly trusted. I turn into the alley, my heart heavy, my arm painful, but my love for Josef carrying me forward.

He'll help me in every way he can, I just need to wait four hours before I visit the drop. Once I have the package in hand, I'll have the resources I need to move ahead.

The bell above the door of the tiny hotel jingles until I grab it and silence it in my palm. The vestibule is dimly lit and warm. It's late. The clerk is sound asleep, snoring, behind the desk on a cot. My key is lying on the counter. A note tied to the ring. "Welcome Mrs. Grayson. See me in the morning."

I've stayed here years ago. Same note. Different fake name. Same clerk. It's why I knew it was safe enough for me to rest for a few hours.

Long enough for a good cry while I change my bandage.

Plenty of time to remember the man who saved my life, held me in his arms, and for some reason, deposited me into an apartment full of spy cameras.

Nothing makes sense.

Except the fact that I was a fool.

I never should have let the gates around my heart open the tiniest amount. It hurts.

So damned bad.

\* \* \*

THE SKY IS FADING from ink to lavender when I open the trash can lid in the park. Pretending to drop in a coffee cup, I see the package. A tattered paper bag with food stains on it.

The coast is clear. I already checked, so I lift the bag and walk slowly away as if I'm about to enjoy a breakfast as the sun rises over the river.

## CHAPTER 16

Sitting on a park bench by the slowly flowing water, I dig into the bag. On top is a breakfast sandwich. Unopened with a smiley face drawn on the paper. Ah. Josef always made sure I was fed.

"You poor child. No one should have to starve like you have," he said the first day he fed me. The day he caught me picking a lock on the grocery store he used as a front for his operation.

While I gobbled up everything he set in front of me, he plied me to learn how I was so skilled at being a thief at the young age of fourteen.

For some reason, having a full belly in that warm break room in the back of his shop turned me into a confession machine.

He didn't like my answers to his questions. The veins in his neck stood out when I told him about being orphaned a year before. Explained how I was surviving off of picking locks and eating garbage.

That was the first day he fed me. And he hasn't stopped since.

The sandwich that I know he made for me by hand has my favorite ingredients. Crusty bread, butter and tomato with salt and pepper. I take a bite, close my eyes and remember eating this same meal at his table many times.

As I eat slowly, savoring the flavors, I look through the items he disguised in pieces of rubbish. A new fake passport. A bundle of cash. Two burner phones. One labeled with the number one in grease marker. The other is unmarked. And of course, he included a set of lock picks, a bug sniffer, and a switchblade—his favorite weapon.

Turning on the bug sniffer, I walk around the park bench and the ten feet surrounding the space. All clear.

Turning on the phone, I dial the only number programmed in it, another burner phone, I'm sure.

"Child. Are you enjoying the sandwich?"

Smiling, I reply, "Very much. Thank you."

"What's going on?"

I tell him the story. Leaving out the part about losing my head and sleeping with my surgeon. I only say that he helped me find what I thought was safe lodging for my recovery. The whole time I talk, he sounds shocked and upset, making deep grumbles and huffs on the other end. "You trusted a doctor? I'm very shocked at this. I know your deep dislike for the medical world."

I set the sandwich aside. "It was a mistake, something foolish. I'm not sure what happened to my head."

"He saved your life. That's hard to ignore."

So is having his blood inside of me.

And knowing I had his seed in my womb.

And the fact that I can still feel all the places he touched me.

Finally, he says, "This man, this shooter, what would his motive be to maim you?"

"That's what I'm unsure of."

"You're going to find him?"

"Of course, didn't you expect me to say that?"

He laughs heartily. "Of course, but I didn't know for certain, you've been playing nanny for some time now, I thought you might have hung up your cloak."

I gasp and chuckle. "Don't say such words. I've just been taking a break."

"Well, it's time to get back to work, isn't it?"

"Indeed. So now, where to start?"

"Take a few days to recover. I'll do some research."

"Thank you so much."

"Dispose of the phone. The other one is clean. You know how to reach me otherwise."

"I do."

As I prepare to hang up, he says, "Child. Wait."

"Yes?"

"My senses are telling me that something big is coming."

"Me too," I whisper. "I'll be in touch, soon, I promise."

## CHAPTER SEVENTEEN

*Scotch*

The cabin lights slowly rise as the aircraft begins its descent. From the cockpit of our private jet, Sierra says, "Welcome to France."

Andre yawns and stretches in his seat across the aisle from me. "That was fast."

"You were out like a light."

Cole walks past us, toward the front of the plane and slides into the co-pilot seat, leaning over to kiss his pregnant wife on the cheek as he takes his spot.

A stab of jealousy hits me. I'm not the jealous type, so it surprises me.

Cole Strong and Sierra have somehow found the perfect life together, unconventional, but perfect. Of course, the Strong brothers are family kind of men. At least, now they are, after they found their ultimate mates.

I'm apparently not the only one that notices. "Cut out the mushy shit," grumbles Andre with a half smirk and shake of his head.

Cole looks over his shoulder with a cocky grin on his rugged face. "Kiss my ass, you jealous S.O.B."

Andre laughs, then glances at me. His expression turns hard, all humor and teasing gone. "We're going to find your girl."

I look away. "She's not my girl. I'd just like to know she's safe. I don't think she has anyone other than the Agile Team."

He crosses one leg over the other. "Tell yourself what you like, she's yours."

"Tell that to two point one million people in Paris. Maybe someone will help us find her."

## CHAPTER EIGHTEEN

*Scotch*

### Nearly One Month Later

I stretch against the smooth cotton sheets. Unsure of the time. Unsure of the date. Uncertain of the place. But it doesn't matter.

The low light of morning slips through the curtain and caresses the gentle curve of Simona's upturned breasts where she's standing across the room from me. She shifts and smiles at me, softly, teasingly, as she pushes her hair back over her shoulder.

I reach for her, motioning her to the bed. Needing to feel her skin. Taste her kiss. Going mad to drive myself into her.

She takes a step toward me as she skims her hands down

## CHAPTER 18

over her bare nipples. Then lower, where she lightly touches herself at the teasingly bare vee of her legs.

*God. I'm one lucky son of a bitch.* Her body is perfection and the way she's looking at me makes me want to roar.

My mouth is suddenly dry. Starving. Dying for her. I lick across my lips, recalling her sweet feminine flavor as blood rushes toward my instant erection. "Come here, angel."

Her smile widens as she holds her hand out for me. "Come and get me, big guy." She breathes the last words as she steps closer, but just out of reach.

A sudden shrill sound jolts me awake.

Simona's image vanishes and I open my eyes as my heart points. In front of me is nothing but the tan wallpaper of a hotel room wall.

My breath ragged, a stampeding buffalo inside of my chest, I snarl, "Faaak!" As I snatch the phone off the nightstand.

Nearly every night for the last month, the siren Simona has invaded my dreams with her seductive body and her teasing words. Sometimes, on the very same nights, I have nightmares about her dying in my hands in the back of that car.

"What?" I snap as I shove a rattled hand in my hair.

Marshall cuts right to the reason for his call. "We have a lead."

I sit bolt upright, pitching the sheet off. "Someone saw her?"

"Someone saw Pavel. And there was a woman tailing him."

"Jesus!" I'm scrambling off the bed, shoving my legs into my jeans. The bedroom door smashes into the wall and back at me when I throw it open. As I storm into the shared sitting room of the suite, I'm yelling. "Andre, get up. Someone spotted Pavel and possibly Simona."

I turn my attention back to the phone. "Where were they?"

"Avenue de l'Opéra. Pavel was buying groceries. A woman, similar build but with dark hair in a black cocktail dress was seen exiting the store and following him for a few blocks, following his turns."

With my heartbeat pounding in my temples, I half yell, "That's fucking amazing. That means he's staying near there."

"Exactly my thought."

Andre's dressed and at the door with his twin holsters full of guns in less than a minute. I toss him the keys to the rented car. If there's one thing the man does, it's drive fast in jacked up city traffic.

It's a quarter to midnight when we make the address where they were last seen. Half hour has passed. A lot can happen in that time. My gut was in a knot, my heart in cardiac arrest the whole drive.

"I'll work the southern blocks," Andre says as he gets out of the car.

I head in the opposite direction. Praying for anything. Any sign. Any clue.

People brush past me, dressed for late dinners or going to bars. Laughing. Talking in French. It's a busy area. Music and traffic noises suffuse the evening air.

For the first few minutes, I feel acutely overstimulated. Like a dog that's been let loose on the hunt. I'm not good in that state.

Something you pick up when you're practicing wartime medicine—You have to slow down to speed up.

I stop, stepping to the edge of the sidewalk, and press

## CHAPTER 18

my back against the brick wall. Taking a few slow breaths, I reach for the calm that I know I have within me. That's when I can do almost superhuman things. When I can tune into the most subtle details.

Four young women, chattering in French, round the corner and pass me. A cloud of expensive perfume trails along behind them. Two of them look back over their shoulders at me, laughing throaty, appreciative laughs, letting their eyes trace over me from foot to head.

They're all in cocktail dresses and impossibly skinny high heels. Obviously, they've been somewhere classy. I'll start there. Maybe Simona was dressed like that for a reason. Maybe she wants to fit in.

Now, to follow them, or go in the direction they're coming from?

The cell phone of one of the women rings. She's talking loud enough for me to hear. I just pray my French is good enough.

Thankfully, she keeps it simple. "Oui, encore deux minutes. Commandez nos boissons, s'il vous plaît." *Yes, just two more minutes. Order our drinks, please.*

Ah, so they are on their way out for the evening. I fall in behind them, keeping plenty of space.

The woman was right. Two minutes later, they're walking into a club-restaurant combo. It's teeming with people. Beautiful. Dressed to kill. I'd never get inside in the jeans, plain black t-shirt, and leather coat I have on. So, I make a turn and cross the street, looking for a place to wait.

But I'm drawn up short when I hear, "Mr. American!"

I'm brisling with annoyance when I turn. The brunette, the one who got the phone call, is standing with her hand on her hip. In accented English, she says, "You want to come inside? I know the owners."

"No, that's not necessary."

She studies me for a moment. "Pity. It would be nice to spend some time with you."

"I'm not looking for—" I forget all about talking to the woman when the crowd parts enough for me to see in through the window. It's her. Simona, sitting on a stool at the end of the bar, close enough to the windows to see outside.

I'd know her anywhere. Even with dark brown hair and thick red lipstick on. I instantly recognize her.

"Actually, yes. I'll come in."

She smiles, a coy smile. "Good. I like American soldier men." She extends her hand and I move toward her as the crowd closes around the front of the building again. The woman pulls me through the throng of boisterous partiers, and into a hallway where the coat check line holds us up. The hostess gives me a hard glare looking over my inappropriate attire. The woman clutching my arm speaks rapidly in French and instantly the face of the hostess changes. Obviously, the owner card has been pulled in this standoff. She smiles victoriously as we flow with the stream of people entering the club.

The second we step into the main room of the building, I pull away. "Excuse me for a minute."

My height has always been an advantage in clubs. And tonight's no different. I don't have to push all the way through the crowd to the bar to know Simona's not on that barstool anymore. The seat is empty.

She's disappeared in a sea of brunettes in black dresses and men with expensive suits. Fuck.

Turning around, I look for the exit. The entrance we used was one way. There has to be another way out of the club. In my broken French, I ask a waitress for the exit. She points toward a wall not far from me.

Maybe…

I weave through traffic and push open the door into a dead-end alley. When I hit the main street at a jog, I catch sight of a woman, long brown hair, black cocktail dress, turning the corner two blocks away. I sprint after her.

Again, I catch a glimpse of her. This time turning into a doorway for an apartment building.

By the time I reach it, she's already inside and the door's locked. Jesus! I jerk my phone out of my pocket and call Andre. "Target spotted, but she went into a building."

"Text me the address."

"Copy, I'm going to see if there's —"

The door pops open and a young couple hurry out onto the sidewalk, never noticing me. I grab the door. "I'm in." I whisper and disconnect.

I stand in the lobby, listening for a few seconds, until I hear heels on tile. Turning toward the sound, I take the stairs as stealthily as I can. I'm going to need the advantage of surprise or she's going to try to lose me again.

I hit the landing and follow her sound again. But when I hear a man's footsteps on the stairs behind me, I turn in the opposite direction of the click of Simona's heels.

Stepping into the shallow door well of an apartment, I conceal myself as best as I can.

The man's footfalls continue up toward me, and turn on the landing toward Simona's direction. I peek around the corner. Son of a bitch. It's Pavel.

In one arm is a bag of groceries. He's unaware of my presence, I'm sure. Which is perfect.

I move after him, quieting my steps. He never sees me

coming. And when I strike him with the edge of my hand in just the right spot on his neck, he doesn't even have time to speak. I catch him, and his bag of groceries before he hits the floor.

Setting the bag aside, I grab the neck of his jacket and drag him down the hallway in the direction Simona went.

As I near the end, I know she has to be close. There's no exit. But I remember I am dealing with Simona, so hard to tell where the hell she is.

"I brought you something," I say into the quiet corridor, loud enough she'd be sure to hear me.

When she steps out of a door well, there's pure fury in her eyes. She stamps her stiletto on the tile. "What in the hell are you doing here?"

"Helping you."

She tips her chin up and burns a whole into my face with her eyes. Through gritted teeth, she bites out her words. "I. Do. Not. Need. Your. Help."

"Maybe you don't, but you got it anyway."

She snarls. "And! And! Who was the French bimbo?"

"Who knows?" I glance at Pavel who's slumbering on the floor, his head lolled to the side. "We should take him inside so we can continue this conversation without the police getting involved."

"I swear!" she mutters as she digs into the tiny purse hanging from her wrist. With quick fingers, she picks the lock on the door of the apartment to my right. "I can't believe you followed me. How did you find me?"

I follow her inside, dragging Pavel's limp body.

She looks at him again. "What did you do to him?"

"Stunned his nervous system with a neck blow. Have any handcuffs?"

"Do I look like I have any handcuffs hidden in my dress?"

# CHAPTER 18

Uh. No, you don't. The only thing hidden under that dress are the beautiful parts of you that I want. I grin, "Nope. Nothing nefarious under that dress for sure."

She slings her purse at me. "Or in there?"

Simona growls and stomps away. I rip off the cord of the nearest lamp and have Pavel's hands bound by the time she comes back with two belts.

She throws them at me. When I'm done binding the man up, I stand. She's still glaring. Fuming. Smoke coming out of her ears, the toe of her sleek black shoe tapping on the floor.

I let my eyes trace over her. Every damned beautiful inch of her. "Fuck, I missed you."

She fists her hands by her sides.

Then flies at me.

I catch her as she throws herself into my arms.

Her voice is shaky. "I don't know whether to kiss you or kill you."

I carry her to the couch and flatten her beneath me as my mouth slams into hers.

Her hands claw at my shirt. When her fingers dig into my skin, a possessive growl starts to rattle in my chest. She spreads her legs wider for me as I push up her dress.

"Damn, hot, *fucking* damn." Beneath the dress, she's bare.

With my teeth, I tear down the thin strap, laying her nipples gloriously exposed for my mouth.

She arches into me when I nip at her delicious pink nipple. Her voice raw and full of lust when she says, "Scotch—Yes. Oh!"

I grind into her. "I've been going mad to find you. I was worried sick"

"You have been?"

"It's a miracle they haven't locked me up."

She smiles against my mouth when I kiss her again. We devour each other. Biting. Licking. Sucking, tangling our tongues together until we both are dizzy and panting.

I rub my throbbing, hungry dick against her wet center. "Thank god your shoulder is better because I'm not feeling gentle tonight."

Moaning deep in her sexy throat, she twists against me. "Neither am I."

When I drive into her, she throws her head back. I slam into her over and over, needing to feel her, needing to hear her.

I thrust and thrust, until we slide off the couch onto the floor, in the narrow space between it and the coffee table. "Oh, god. I'm close—"

Her fingers shake as she wraps her hands around my face. I tumble headfirst into her eyes. Losing myself fast and hard. I slow my strokes, lean down and kiss her. "Come for me, babe, come and show me how much you missed me."

Her lashes mist as she nods. Slipping my hand between us, I locate her clit. With concerted strokes and pressure, I drive her to the brink.

Her breath hitches, her legs shake against me. And I don't stop. I keep the same angle, the same speed, the same pressure.

The climax hits her and she shrieks, bucking hard against me, and I couldn't stop my orgasm if I had to. I follow with a deep throat shredding growl. When I'm spent, I drop down onto her, making sure to keep my full weight off her small body.

She wraps her arms around my neck. "You came for me."

"I came for you. Then I came in you."

She grins. "You're full of yourself."

"You're full of me."

She rolls her eyes. "Good lord, help me."

I kiss the tip of her nose. The curve of her brow. The corner of her sexy lips.

A groan in the entryway of the apartment makes me stiffen. I push up off her. Hating the fact that I have to pull out. But there's something big and ugly that needs to be taken care of.

"What was that?" she says, alarm on her face as I rearrange my cock back into my pants.

"A dead man, moaning."

She scrambles up, fighting her dress. "No! Don't kill him!"

"He fucking shot you. Point blank." I start jerking open kitchen drawers.

"God, what are you looking for?"

"A knife. A big, fucking, sharp knife."

"What?" she shrieks as she stares at me in horror.

I hold up a big cleaver. "This should do."

Simona makes a squeak, her eyes roll back in her head and she falls to the floor in a dead faint.

## CHAPTER NINETEEN

## Simona

There's a really bright light in my eyes. I blink. Groan. *Ugh.*

"Wake up, beautiful."

"Huh? What?"

Scotch, wearing a worried expression, is leaning over me. "You fainted."

"Oh."

I stretch. That's when I realize I'm wearing a dress. My legs are bare and cold. I lift my head and look down at myself, puzzled by my attire.

"Take it easy. How are you feeling?"

"Confused." I lick across my lips. A fuzzy memory surfaces. Then I feel all of the tender places inside of me and my memory comes flooding back. "Wait—"

Scotch pushes my hair back. "Remember?"

"Yes."

## CHAPTER 19

"The knife?"

I nod. "You didn't chop him up, did you?"

Narrowing those dark brows of his, he says, "Not yet. But I'm going to."

"You wouldn't..."

He grins darkly. "Without a second thought."

I try to sit up. "Help me."

With a giant hand, Scotch levers me up and props me against the couch. "Don't move. Sit here and get your body adjusted to being upright."

*Ugh.* I moan as my stomach tries to revolt. "I feel ill."

He rises and disappears into the bathroom. A few seconds later, he comes back with a cool, wet towel.

I swipe it over my face for a couple of minutes. When the nausea passes, I find my voice. "We have to talk. You can't kill Pavel until I find out what his motive was for the shooting."

Scotch's face turns hard. "I don't really care what his motive was."

"I do. It might be important."

With murderous eyes, Scotch says, "If he's dead, it won't matter."

I shake my head. "Stop being a caveman. In the intelligence world, you have to know when to off your target. When they've outlived their usefulness. Right now, I need him alive."

"I'll feel better when he's dead."

"I thought you saved lives. Not took them."

He looks affronted, suddenly. "You don't seem to understand. It wrecked me to see him shoot you. I haven't stopped thinking about having your blood all over me for the last month. I won't let it happen again."

I reach for his handsome face. "You're kind of freaking me out."

"I've been wrecked, not knowing if you were okay. Not knowing if that fuckface found you again."

"I'm sorry," I whisper.

"It destroyed me when you ran. The Agile team has been on the hunt ever since. What spooked you so bad you had to run from everyone?"

I look away.

He catches my chin and turns me back to face him. "What spooked you?"

"The apartment was full of cameras. As soon as I found them, a man showed up at the door."

"Full of cameras, what do you mean?"

"The bedroom, I found two and that's without even doing a thorough search."

"You think I took you to an apartment that I knew was bugged?"

"I didn't know. What was I supposed to think?"

He fumbles in his pocket for his phone. A few seconds later, it's ringing and on speaker phone. "Will, what the fuck do you have cameras in your apartment bedroom for?"

There's a pause on the other end of the line. "Uh, yeah. Well, Mindy and I stream our sex live on the internet."

Scotch is pissed. His color is hot, the vein in his forehead is thick and pulsing. "Where else do you have cameras?"

"A couple in the kitchen and a couple in the living room. Oh, and the security camera on the door, both inside and out."

I can't hold my tongue any longer. "Did Scotch know about any of that before now?"

## CHAPTER 19

Listening for any telltale signs of the man lying. I wait. But not long. He says, "God, no. No way. I mean, I told him about the security camera on the door because that's how I knew his girl had gotten scared and taken off. I called him the minute the security system notified me of someone knocking on the door."

Scotch watches my face as I listen. When his friend and I fall silent, Scotch says, "Will, meet Simona. The girl from the videos."

"Jesus. You finally found her! I know you were going apeshit."

"I did. Now, we have a lot to talk about, but you've helped clear up one problem."

"Shit, I hope so. And I'm sorry if the cameras freaked you out. I hide them so Mindy doesn't look at them while we're having sex. We get a lot more likes and make a lot more money off the videos when they are more... authentic."

Scotch shakes his head. "You're fucking rich already. Why the hell are you selling bedroom porn?"

Will laughs. "Because it's fun. Our sex is hot as hell. Why not make a little play money at it."

"I'm going now," Scotch says and he disconnects.

"Weird friend."

"He is. Don't let that be a representation of the kind of person I am."

I reach for him, grab his hand. "Thank you for calling him. It makes more sense now."

"Good. Now let's get back to the important topic of cutting off body parts and putting that bastard down the garbage chute."

I close my eyes and count to ten. "No. We are not."

"Weren't you going to kill him anyway?"

"I'm not sure. I've kind of lost my taste for blood. I don't know why, but I haven't decided yet what to do with him. I'll tell you later. Now, help me up. I've got some interrogation to do."

# CHAPTER TWENTY

*Scotch*

Simona, small, but stronger than she looks, rolls Pavel onto his side. She jerks on his ear as she shakes him. "Wake up!"

Pavel blinks and groans. "Who the hell?"

"It's me. Remember? The one you shot!"

His eyes pinwheel around, then land on me before he jerks them away. Simona snaps her fingers right in front of Pavel's face. "Hey, buddy. Right here."

I drop down on my haunches. "You almost killed her, you son of a bitch. And you're going to pay."

The ugly sucker's face blanches whiter.

"Why did you shoot me?"

Pavel swallows, clears his throat as I give him a murderous glare.

"I... I didn't want your team to get the hostage. She was very valuable."

Simona crosses her arms. "Same slimeball you always were, huh? Working for the highest dollar, be damned of the consequences."

In a rough voice, he says, "I need the money."

He scowls at her as if his answer justifies any horrible thing he might do. "Me mum. I take care of her. She needs a surgery that cannot be done here."

Simona pushes up to her feet. "That's so nice, Pavel. I'm sure she's real proud of you. Now, let's cut through the chase, I know you've been trying to find me. I accessed your internet searches and didn't like what I saw."

He instantly replies, "I wanted to see if you lived."

On bare feet, she paces across the narrow apartment, clenching and unclenching her fists. "So, let me see here, Pavel. You suddenly care if I live after you shot me in a third world country? I don't buy it."

She stops and pivots. I can see the wheels turning in her head as she pushes her now dark brown hair back. "And the really troubling part is that you were searching for me before you saw me in San Miguel."

My hackles stand up instantly. What the hell? "Did you know she was going to be in San Miguel?"

A bead of sweat runs down Pavel's forehead and into his eye.

"Did you?" I yell right in his face.

"No. No! I didn't. It was a coincidence."

I grab the man and yank him up to his knees even though his hands and feet are still tied behind him. I growl, my anger barely restrained. "You need to start talking now."

Simona paces past us. "Why would you be looking for me? I'm not in the business anymore, so I know it's not for the reasons our paths crossed in the past. So, what is it?"

Pavel looks far too comfortable for my taste. "You've got

## CHAPTER 20

five seconds to answer. Five. Four... Did you know that the human eyeball can be removed with the flick of one finger?"

His throat works nervously. That's better.

"Three. Did you know that a human trachea can be crushed with two fingers? Two."

Pavel croaks, "Who is this crazy person?"

Simona glances my way, "Oh, just the surgeon that wants to chop you up with a cleaver and dump you down the trash chute."

The man whimpers and nearly topples over. I take the opportunity to lift the gigantic cleaver off the floor. Just to drive home how much trouble he's in.

"Okay! Okay, alright. I'll tell you."

Simona drops onto the nearby chair and crosses one leg over the other. "All of it. Get on with it."

With his lip quivering, Pavel says, "Make him put the cleaver away. P-please."

Simona shakes her head. "Nah. But get on with it. I don't have all night. I have somewhere to be."

Keeping an eye on me, the man clears his throat. "There's a bounty for you."

She waves her hand dismissively. "I'm not surprised. I did, after all, ruin many people's day when I was working."

"No. It's not that at all. This is a very big bounty. And not for your murder. For your return to someone. Your owner."

She stiffens, her jaw hardening, and she snaps, "Make yourself clear."

"There is a man looking for you. And others. Apparently, you are very important to him. The reward is far more than any job I've ever taken."

I step in his line of sight, "Who's looking for her?"

"A man, his name has been protected. And he didn't

even know her name. But when I learned about the birthmark, I remembered you have it. I always thought that mark was strange. I knew it was you. The age, the home country, and the complexion match the description the man has given. That mark is confirmation of your identity. Apparently, your birthmark proves you are his."

As soon as the word 'birthmark' leaves his mouth, I know exactly the thing he's talking about. The crescent moon shaped mark on her cheek. A most unusual mark. Almost like a mole, cocoa in color, but perfectly shaped.

Simona's as still as a stone column. Her eyes laser focused on the man, but I can feel her growing distant. She's retracting into some deep hollow space.

Her fingers rise to her cheek and touch the place where that odd moon sits.

I grab Pavel's hair and yank his face up. "How much money is being offered?"

"T-Two million."

Ice runs through my chest and into every one of my extremities.

Holy mother of disaster. For two million dollars, every piece of crap in the world would look for her.

My voice is hard and uncompromising. "You're going to give us everything. All of the details! Do you hear me? You do, and I'll make sure your mother gets whatever care she needs. If I find out you've omitted anything, she won't have a son to take care of her. Do you *UNDERSTAND*?"

He tries to nod, but can't. He croaks out his reply. "*Yes. Yes. I will.*"

I drop my hold on his head and go to Simona's side. When I kneel down next to her, she's almost completely shut down. Eyes glassy, face dangerously blank. She has the weight of something in her expression that I can't fathom. I

## CHAPTER 20

grip her shoulder. "Hey, why don't you go get some water, take a break. Look for something warmer to put on. I think we're going to be here a while."

When she doesn't move, I use her hand to pull her up. "Let's get you out of here for a few minutes."

Over my shoulder, I warn, "Pavel. I know all the ways to hurt you that won't kill you. Keep that in mind in case you have the urge to try to get away."

He half groans, half whimpers as Simona follows me down the corridor of the narrow apartment. I turn into the bathroom, pulling her in behind me. The door closes with a squeak.

Jesus. What a mind-fuck. It wrecks me to feel her shivering when I pull her into my arms. "You're not alone."

With surprising force, she throws her arms around me.

I kiss the top of her head. "It's okay. We'll figure this out together."

## CHAPTER TWENTY-ONE

# Simona

The cold tile burns at my bare feet. But the warmth of Scotch's strong arms offers the only solace I know I'll find in the midst of this jacked up situation.

So, I let him hold me, too stunned to talk. Too terrified to admit that I am being hunted.

It was one thing to be chased when I was a spy... that was part of the game. This, somehow, feels different. I'm not to be killed. I'm to be collected.

For someone who says he owns me.

When I finally find my voice, it's bitter and cold. "I don't belong to anyone."

Scotch smooths his hand down my hair. "No, you don't, babe."

"I'm disturbed that I carry some kind of recognizable mark..."

Scotch tilts my face up and sternly studies the mark on

my cheek. I wondered about this little moon. It's perfect. Almost too perfect for a natural mark. His calloused thumb rubs over it again. "It's a natural birthmark. Unique, though."

Clenching his t-shirt, I feel myself swaying.

The worry in Scotch's face grows. And the fear and uncertainty inside of me take on a life of their own. Consuming me from the tip of my cold toes to the top of my crawling scalp.

He pulls me tighter, nestling me in his strength. When he lets me go, he sheds his black leather coat and wraps it around me. "Are you okay enough to continue? If you don't want to, I can take it from here."

I push a shaky hand into my bottle-brown hair. He brushes his lips across my temple as his arms band around me.

"No. I want to hear everything."

He reaches into the pocket of his jacket and pulls out his cell phone, suddenly. "I need to check in with the team. Andre's on the streets looking for you. Everyone's been worried sick."

My chest squeezes with guilt. It's an unfamiliar sensation. So many years on my own. Hiding. Working in stealth. You never get too close to anyone.

Watching my face as if he's reading me, he leans down and plants a swift kiss. "Don't let him scare you. I'm here with you now, the Agile Team is ready to do whatever we need them to do. We'll kick those sons of bitches to Antarctica and back."

The ferocity in his voice does something to me. It bolsters me. And it makes me want something with this man that I shouldn't. A future.

Because I might not have one to share.

And if I do, would I even know how to do that?

My examples of love and relationships are zilch.

But that doesn't matter right now.

I push everything else out of my mind when Scotch opens the door. He follows me down the hallway to where Pavel's sitting on his knees, hands and feet tied behind him, with his head hung low.

I take the seat on the chair nearby again because my knees are woozy-feeling. "Pavel, so, tell me about this bounty."

With bloodshot eyes, he looks me over. It's a look that makes my skin crawl.

Scotch snarls, "Keep your fucking eyes down."

Instantly, Pavel snaps his eyes to the floor.

"There's not much more to tell. The job is to find you and two other people. Two million dollars for each one."

My wheels spin, three people? "How did you hear about this?"

"The dark web. It was in some of the chatrooms."

Scotch shifts and folds his arms across his chest. "How many people were talking about hunting Simona?"

"A handful. But I think I'm the only one who knew who she is. Unless someone is keeping it close to their chest. Everyone else is just on a wild goose chase hoping to run across a woman of your age, origin country, and general physical description with the birthmark."

I ask, "Was there a picture of the birthmark?"

"Yeah. There was. A small image. I think it was on a man's face, though. You know how the holes in the skin look different?" He glances at Scotch.

Scotch says, "The pores, you mean?"

"That's it. I'm not into facials or lotions and the like, so they are just holes to me."

Scotch narrows his eyes. "So, who was hiring?"

"Everyone in those forums has a fake persona, just an avatar. It would be damned hard to figure out who it really is."

I lean in, steepling my fingers. "But if you find me, how are you supposed to connect with the person who's paying?"

Pavel shrugs, but doesn't look at me. "Generally, I mean, you know this, there's a way to send a message to the person through the forum. This job requires proof of capture and proof of the fact that you are alive. Then an exchange will be arranged."

A shudder runs through me. "What else do I need to know?"

For a split second, his eyes flip up to mine, then to Scotch. "You know, I'm not the only one who's seen that mole. Including him." He tips his chin at Scotch. "He could decide to turn you over for a big fat paycheck."

Lethally calm, voice pitched low, Scotch says, "Enough." He looks over to me. "You might want to leave the room."

I leap to my feet with my heart trying to escape through my throat. "Wait." I'm shaking all over as Scotch's ferocious protectiveness rocks my marrow.

Drawing a shaky breath, I get my fire back. "Hold on. I've got an idea. He needs to have all his body parts working for this."

The grimace on Pavel's face fades, just a smidge. Scotch, though, he's having none of it. If the man could shred steel and concrete with his stare, this whole building would crumble.

I rest a hand on his forearm with pleading in my eyes. "Just listen."

We stare off. Finally, he gives in. Offers just a quick,

very small nod. I turn back to Pavel. "Now, what I'm going to say is in addition to what my friend here offered for your mother. So, listen up. Since your plan to get the money for me is shot, I have an offer. I'll pay you ten thousand dollars to go back to the forum and dig around for information on the other two people that are being hunted."

Scotch makes a sound close to a growl.

I brace myself for the reaction he's going to have to what I say next. "And I'll pay you another 5k to take me to the guy, as part of a trap."

Pavel's eyes saucer and his mouth quirks into a weird grin.

The sound that comes from Scotch's chest is something I didn't know a human could make. Half bear, half raging lion. It sends a chill to the very base of my spine that snaps me upright.

Oh no, he doesn't. He can't use that tactic to make me back down.

Nope. Not letting him dictate what I do. Ever.

## CHAPTER TWENTY-TWO

*Scotch*

The second Andre sees my face, he knows there's something serious going down. He mutters, "Frickin-A," and swipes his hand over his three-day-old beard shadow.

Holding the door to Pavel's apartment open, I tip my head toward the living room. He steps into the small space and stalks toward the bound and tied prisoner. He lets out a huff. "Damn, Sprite. Talk about a wild fucking goose chase. Paris? I mean, could you two pick anywhere more complicated for finding someone?"

Thoroughly undisturbed, Simona waves a dismissive hand. "The food's good, at least. It could have been much, much worse."

He steps toward her and captures her in a bear hug. "Damn, it's good to see you have your attitude back."

"Well, it's good to see you too."

She glances at me over his shoulder but won't hold my gaze.

For the last ten minutes, she's been like that while we waited for Andre and she talked some nonsense bullshit about using herself to trap whoever has a bounty on her.

Fuck. That. Craziness.

If she thinks I'm letting her be any kind of damned decoy, or trap, or whatever the hell she thinks she's going to be, she's wrong. *Dead wrong.* No freaking way. Wrong.

And I don't care how mad she is, because I can't spend another minute thinking about her being in danger.

And that's where Agile is going to come in. Andre and the team know the deal. Or at least, enough of it to keep up their end of it.

The rest, we have to figure out when we can all sit down and make some sense out of what Pavel has told us.

Andre lurches toward Pavel and with those gigantic hands of his, he hoists him up off the floor. A flash of light bounces off Andre's knife as he cuts the restraints. He pushes the man toward the door. "Let's go have a little talk."

Simona's eyes go wide. Panic blanches her skin. "Where are you going?"

"Unfinished business related to the other kidnapping." Andre tosses over his shoulder as he marches Pavel into the hallway.

Simona's mouth drops open. Then she slams it shut. "Don't kill him!"

"Don't worry, I've been given strict orders not to do too much damage."

Crossing her arms, she huffs. "What about his mother? Scotch is supposed to help her."

Pavel yells an address as Andre continues to push him down the hallway, farther from the man's apartment. The

## CHAPTER 22

sound of the two men's boots disappears down the stairwell a few seconds later.

And I'm left with an angry brunette in a skin tight black dress glaring a hole in the middle of my chest.

*Meh.* What's new?

Such is life with Simona. And I wouldn't have her any other way. Well, except naked.

Which is my next plan.

"Come on. Let's go to the hotel. We have a lot to talk about."

With a little snarl, my tiny hellcat unleashes on me. "Jameson Scott. I've never been so mad in my life. A talk? We have nothing to talk about unless you're the one talking and you're telling me you're going to stay out of my business."

She's within arm's reach. For me, anyway. I have the wingspan of an NBA player. I catch her, looping my palm around the back of her neck and slide my fingers up into her silky hair. "Not going to happen, beautiful. As a matter of fact, I'm pretty sure I'm about to be even farther inside your business. *Deep,* deep inside your business."

I've never seen her eyes flare so hot. "*You!* You arrogant, pig headed, cocky–"

When I smash my lips against hers, she tries to bite me. I tip my head back and laugh. That's when her fists come up and start to hammer against my chest, but I catch her wrists.

"Hold onto all that frustration, little one. Take that out on me in a bit. When we're naked and can make a wreck out of the hotel bed."

She freezes. And I take advantage of her dismay, or shock, or whatever the hell it is. I grab her ass and jerk her up against my rock-hard cock. "It drives me mad when you're all feisty. Did you know that, Sprite?"

Color suffuses her cheeks, and I steal another kiss. "Now, get those sexy as sin shoes of yours on. We've got a date with a bottle of lube and a silk scarf."

She gasps and stammers back when I let her hands go. I laugh harder this time. "You're lying."

I smack her butt. "I'm not. While I was chasing your ass all over Paris, I stumbled upon a sex shop. And I bought a few things."

She swipes her shoes off the floor, and for a second, I wonder if she might use the lethal looking things as weapons against me. But then she puts them on, one by one, on her slender, sexy feet. "You were so sure you'd find me. *AND* that I'd have something to do with you... "

Looping my arm around her, I lead her to the door. "Babe, when you know, you know."

## CHAPTER TWENTY-THREE

## Simona

Waving a hand, Scotch easily hails a taxi. It's late and the streets are much quieter now as we zip across Paris. Tucked in the back of the little cab. Deep in the dark interior with the city's glittering lights flying by.

For some reason, I can't pull myself away from his side.

It's like I've been sucked into some kind of Scotch vortex and can't get free.

*Lord.* How he makes me fume.

Almost as much as he makes me want.

It's ridiculous. The way he turns me inside out. Upside down. Wrong side in. Argh!

But the man does it for me. Against all reason.

All that bulging muscle, long-limbed confidence, and the sense of humor that always rocks me, every damned time.

Oh, and did I mention the way he holds me?

Nope?

Never in my life has a man held me so strongly. So totally. He makes me feel protected... and L—

No. I can't even think the L word.

It's wrong. So wrong. I can't L.

I just can't. It's not bred into me. Hell, it was frightened out of me.

Twisting my hand in his, I fret over this disturbing realization.

I'm not capable of L.

It never hit so hard before. It was always a vague hypothetical that was the fodder for paperback book covers in the grocery store aisle. For songs on the radio and movies that I was sure were somehow written to sell boxes of tissue.

But this. This is whole next level of terror.

When Scotch brushes his mouth against my ear and murmurs, "My world feels right again with you in my arms," I freeze.

I almost make a horrible EEEP sound.

When I get my chest working again, I'm in full panic. Sensing my unease, Scotch chuckles. A deep rumble in his broad chest. "That was an interesting response."

I spin on the leather bench and grab the back of the seat with one hand. "You can't just say things like that. I'm unprepared. I can't reciprocate or whatever the hell they call that in English."

He smiles that sexy, disarming smile of his and brushes a knuckle down my cheek. "Babe."

"Scotch. Listen. I'm not that girl. I've got a broken L past. My parents destroyed any and all hope of me ever having a functional relationship."

He leans toward me. And before I can pull some hidden lever and eject myself from the cab, he kisses me. Just enough to remind me that my body is fully onboard with any and all madness that has to do with Jameson Scott, M.D..

I gasp for air when he lets me loose.

*Okay,* when I do my part in ending the kiss too, because maybe I was in on it as well. Fifty percent.

"Look, this is serious." I grab his arm and squeeze it hard, as if the sheer pressure of my grip will convey the depth of disturbance he's caused me.

"I don't know what your past is, but you need to know this about me. I'm not made for L—, you know the word. Anyway, I'm the girl that had a father that left his wife and daughter out of pure anger. Boiling with hate, bitterness, and contempt, he was a walking time-bomb. Whatever happened between my parents was a seething, ugly thing that fouled both of their lives and tainted me forever."

Scotch simply curls his fingers with mine, tangling them up as he listens.

I sigh as I prepare to dump everything ugly out there for his good. "I was young but I knew too much. Even if I didn't fully understand what was happening. Within a year of leaving, he lost a street fight to a monster. And... well, he paid the ultimate price."

His steady brown gaze holds mine. "I'm sorry, Simona. That's a terrible thing to experience."

I shake my head. "That's not all. My mother spiraled down into one crisis after another. Finally, one day, eleven months later, I was called from class." I take a shaky breath. "No thirteen-year-old should be told her mother's dead in the cold concrete hallway of school."

But it didn't surprise me. It seemed to fit with the way my life always was. Stark. Cold. Starved for the most basic human kindnesses.

Some part of me wants to shock Scotch. To scare him away. To show him how totally messed up I am, so I tell him the rest of the ugly truth. "I was already digging in the garbage for food by that point. Mom wasn't really a mother anymore. And if I wanted to eat, I had to take care of it. After she died that day, living on the street wasn't much of a stretch. So, when I walked out of the school that day, I never went back to the tiny dingy apartment where my life had been living hell. She was gone. I was gone too."

Scotch is so much stronger than me, I wouldn't be able to resist him pulling me onto his lap. Even if I wanted to.

He's silent for a long time as the driver carves his way across the most romantic city in the world. When he finally speaks, his voice is like warm, golden honey soothing my jangling nerves. "So much makes sense now."

I laugh, it sounds a little bitter. "So, the doctor has me all figured out. What makes sense now?"

"Your fierce independence."

I bury my head in his shoulder. "It's a defense mechanism."

"We all have them."

He might say that, but I have yet to see what his might be.

The cab pulls to a stop in front of a simple hotel. Scotch helps me out, offers his arm. He's unusually quiet as we cross the lobby and ride the small lift.

When he opens the door to a suite, he says, "My room is to the right."

"Andre's staying here too?"

"Yes, we've been here for almost a month."

"I'm sorry."

Scotch slips the jacket from my shoulders. "You were worth the wait."

## CHAPTER 23

I shake my head. "Are you sure? Even if I can't... I'm not capable of love..."

I nearly have to choke the word out. After swallowing my suddenly fat tongue, I say, "Can you just see this as a fling?"

When he turns to look at me, his expression is more serious than any time before. Holding perfectly still, he says in a rough voice, "You were never just a fling. I don't want to put pressure on you to be or do something you don't want. But you need to know too, I come with my own fucked up experience with relationships. And I don't know what the hell the future looks like, but I know that tonight I want to love you."

# CHAPTER TWENTY-FOUR

## Scotch

When Simona steps into my arms, I nearly fall to the ground offering an Amen to whoever got me here. Right here. In this hotel room with her in my arms.

If I only get another night, I only get that. But I know I want so much more. Even if I am as uncertain in the relationship department as she is.

"I haven't told you, but you make a beautiful brunette."

She smiles against my chest. I feel the shape of her cheek change against me. "I love disguises. How did you know it was me?"

"I'd never not know it was you." I lift her and carry her toward the big king size bed. "I'm like a homing pigeon. I'll always be able to find you."

She laughs, full throated and sexy as hell at that.

"Homing pigeons aren't very sexy. Maybe more like a faithful Saint Bernard."

I'm grinning as I take her slinky black dress off. All the way off, unlike when I took her hard and fast on that asshole Pavel's couch.

She watches as I swallow and lick my lips. "If you aren't a sight, I don't know what is."

"As are you, sexy man. Now take off your clothes. Please. Because I'd like to be reminded of how nice the view is below you."

I'm naked in four seconds.

"That's better," she purrs. "Now, what's this talk of lube and silk scarves?"

I reach for the nightstand drawer. "And a few other toys. Which I'm curious to see if you like."

Her eyes widen when she sees the long black scarf, a small bottle of lube, a fingertip vibrator, and the small plug I bought.

She nibbles her lip. "Oh heavens."

"Know what these are?"

"Of course I know what a vibrator is, and the scarf, sure. But the toy... that's something I know only in theory."

I plant my hand beside her head on the bed and lean down to kiss her sexy pink mouth. The mouth I have lots of plans for. "If you're curious, we can play. If not, it's no big deal."

"Will you make me feel as good as the other times we've... you know, when we've...?"

I chuckle at her sudden shyness. "When we've had sex?"

She relaxes a little as if that three-letter word is much more palatable. "Yeah, sex."

"Even better," I promise as I reach for her taut nipple

and pinch it easily between my fingers. She arches against me. Moans my name.

"Somehow, I have a feeling you know what to do. You are the doctor after all."

She goes quiet as I move my hand from one breast to the next while I nip along the cord of her neck.

"So, does the little vixen spy have any secrets for the bedroom?"

A sly smile tips up her lips. "I can hide the cameras far better than your friend."

I just look at her for a beat before I break out into a hearty laugh. She starts giggling.

"God. I L— I mean, I freaking adore you. I'm so glad to know you have some handy skills in case we ever want to set up an Only Fans account."

She reaches for my face, skims her palm along my jaw, letting my days old stubble scrape against her skin. "Why do they call you Scotch?"

"Jameson is a kind of whiskey. Someone decided Scotch was a good nickname in my Navy days. It stuck."

"It fits. For some reason, I always feel like I'm a little drunk, and a lot reckless, when I'm around you."

"Do you think Scotch and Sprite go well together?"

"Just fine," she says as she reaches between us and wraps her delicate hand around my girth. "Better than fine, actually. It's my new favorite cocktail."

# CHAPTER TWENTY-FIVE

*Scotch*

The skin of Simona's inner thigh is made of pale, cream velvet. Rubbing my palm across it, I fight the rush of possessiveness that will make me go too fast.

I want this to last. Forever.

Simona shifts and spreads her beautiful legs wide for me as our tongues fuck like mad. Her hand works magic on my cock as I hover above her, working her up with my mouth, my thumb on her clit.

"I can't wait any more." She breathes and shudders. "I need to feel you."

"Not yet, my dear."

"Argh!" She moans. "Come on..."

Her anguished expression changes to a sweet, tempting smile when I drag the black scarf across her nipples. She doesn't protest a bit when I tie her wrists together. That surprises me, given her need for control. Little by little, she's surrendering her pleasure to me which makes my dick hard as concrete.

"Don't move your arms. Let's see if we can't get you really hot."

"If I get any hotter, I'll melt."

I smile against her nipple. "Perfect." Then I drip three little drops of lube on her clit. Her thighs squeeze against me. "Oh, that's cold."

"Not for long."

I slip the vibrator on my middle finger and run it over her beautiful smooth folds.

Her throat works, and she shifts against me.

"Like that?"

"Yes..."

Moving my other hand to her vee, I spread the lube all around, coating everything. *Everything* from the perfect little clit to the sweet rosebud in the back.

My heart jackhammers as I dip my fingers in her pussy. "So hot. My kitten. My heavens..."

"Scotch... yes, oh. Oh. That's—" She suddenly stops when my thumb glides over her tight little pucker. "Wait. Scotch, I'm a... uh... an anal newby."

I'll admit, hearing that does something primal to me. Watching her expressions carefully, I ask, "Would you like to change that? We can go slow. Just play around with the toy if you want."

She's nervous. I've started to pick up on her tell. A little shift in the shape of her brow. Just barely perceptible, except to a man like me who has made studying her beauty his pastime. "It will feel good, right?"

"I'm not a woman, but it's been known to thrill." I lean

## CHAPTER 25

down and catch her mouth. "Relax. Tell me to stop any time."

She nods, "You've never given me any reason to doubt you. Now, if you would, please, I'd like to come. Or I'm going to choke you with this scarf."

Laughing, because I love her firecracker attitude, I lean down and nibble her thigh as I glide the small vibrator over her clit. Everything about the way she moves tells me it feels good. She wiggles and her breath hitches as I move my thumb over her pussy lips and lower. "That's it. Relax. Just breathe."

Her delicious sweet juices coat my thumb as I press it into the edge of her slit. "So beautiful, just perfect. Rose pink. Hot. Tight as fuck."

I bring her close, but stop short of her orgasm. "Right there, babe, feel that edge. You're ready. I'm going to tease you with the toy."

Flexing her hands against the scarf, her head tosses to the side. Squeezing her eyes tight, she rasps, "Please... Please do anything. I'm *dying* here!"

I tease her with my fingertip first, lubing her up nice and slippery. She shudders. "My god! Okay. All I can say is wow and you haven't even...."

"That's it, babe, it only gets better." Slipping the toy against her, I let her feel the cool silicone. "I'll go slow."

"I'm ready—I think I'm ready. I'm going to die if you don't get me off."

I reposition myself between her thighs, opening her wider, then I begin the systematic unraveling of her control. Clit to pussy, I smooth the vibrator through her wetness and begin to apply gentle pressure to her back entrance with the small toy.

Her breath catches, her lips part, and the pink tip of her

tongue darts out. As I slide the toy inside for the first time, she holds me locked in that crystal-blue stare.

God. She's so beautiful. Wild. Hair tossed about. Lips parted on her little moans.

I want to be where that toy is, but that... that's a whole different animal. We'll have to work up to that slowly.

When I shift so that my fingers can penetrate her pussy too, the first cry tears from her throat.

"Fuck, Simona. That sound undoes me."

Flushed with pleasure, panting, and devouring me with her otherworldly blue eyes, she shudders.

I smile. Viciously. Because I'm fucking exploding with greedy happiness.

And then she lets go.

Her scream is so loud. So long. So incredibly sexy that I nearly come. Almost jet my load all over her perfect tits without even getting inside of her sweet little body.

Her whole being is still shaking when she rasps, "More. I want you, Jameson. Deep inside of my throbbing pussy. Now. *Now.* Now."

Holy madness. *This* woman...

Animal. Vixen.

My destruction. My salvation.

## CHAPTER TWENTY-SIX

*Scotch*

Sounds from the street whisper through the window glass into the blackness of the room. Paris is alive out there, but I want to freeze the moment inside. Just the two of us.

Simona, soft, warm, sleeping soundly, is tucked against my side.

If only my brain wasn't spinning out in a thousand directions with as many questions.

Who is this small, vicious, playful, badass woman?

How have I gotten myself in such a deep mess so quickly?

And I'm not talking about the mess with her and the ugly son of a bitch and whoever is on her trail. I'm talking about the mess of wanting something neither of us is likely capable of offering. Or receiving.

Somehow, in these days, weeks since we've met, it's

been like a time warp with her as my only focus. But this isn't real life.

Cohabitation. Shared checking accounts. Mortgages. Those are real life.

My heart skips behind my sternum. Fuck. *Me.* I'm not cut out for those things. I can do a lot of things. Being a husband and a father aren't two of them.

And a thousand dollars says Simona isn't either.

Once upon a time I dreamed of the whole enchilada.

For about ten minutes.

Then I realized it wasn't going to happen with me serving in the military. That kind of career and marriages and families don't mix. I'd witnessed that firsthand as the child of a single father who tried two times to "marry me a new mother."

Yeah. Bad idea.

*But you're out of the service now.* Reminds my rational brain. But I know I'm not the settling down kind. Hell. Stopping in Eden was my idea of trying it out.

Which has been fine for a few months. Only, I know it's got to have an expiration date. I get itchy. Claustrophobic. And being a plus one isn't conducive to pulling up stakes and seeking out the next right thing.

When the hallway door to the suite opens and closes quietly, my body goes rigid. Holding my breath, I listen hard at the darkness. "It's me," rumbles Andre.

Slowly, I let out my breath and tell my body to relax. But I can't sleep. Not now. Not who knows when. There's too much happening inside my head to really let go.

More than one part of me worries that this thing between us is on a crash course to heartbreak city.

Being super careful, I ease my arm from below Simona. She stirs, stretches. "Are you getting up?"

## CHAPTER 26

"Yeah. I'll be back."

She turns over and curls up into a little ball under the blankets. "Put the light on, please. Leave a gun. I don't sleep well without."

Standing by the bed, I just look at her little form below the thick duvet. My heart spasms sharply. Pieces fall into place—she can't sleep without the lights on.

Her scars run deep. Hidden from the rest of the world. I can't imagine how hard her life has been.

I climb over to her and brush her temple with my lips. "I'll just be in the sitting room. I promise. One of my pistols is on the dresser. I'll turn the light on too."

"K...thank you." She nods sleepily and burrows under the blankets.

Andre's pouring something dark that smells like high test gas into a short glass when I close the bedroom door. He glances my way and back at his drink, something unreadable on his face.

I sit on the end of the chaise lounge as I stretch my tired shoulders. "How did it go?"

"He talked plenty. Guy's nothing but a mercenary for the highest bidder. Scumbag."

"You believe it was a coincidence he ran into her in San Miguel?"

"Yep. And he said he shot her because he needed to slow us down, which we guessed. What we didn't know then was that he did it because it would slow Simona down and hopefully make it easier for him to find her while she recovered."

The bones in my neck creak from how tight the muscles go along my spine. "What kind of bastard shoots a woman like that?"

The darkness of Andre's pupils spreads and the man

transforms into the kind of evil that you'd hate to meet in the alley. But his voice is casual. Which makes him even more dangerous. "The kind with two broken legs."

I blink a few times as I watch him walk to the couch and lower his big frame down to the edge. Andre isn't the kind of man to mince words. But I'm not one hundred percent sure what I'm hearing.

"Your expression says you're not sure if I'm serious." He swirls his glass, throws back a triple shot. "He's still breathing, there's no brain damage, and his arms work just fine. Don't worry."

"What happened?"

"He said the wrong thing. I took care of it. Figured you'd want to do the same."

Part of me wants to know what Pavel said. Part of me knows better than to ask. Finally, I grind out, "Thanks, man."

He stretches an arm onto the back of the couch. "Think nothing of it."

But I do think a lot of it.

As he sits in silence, I fix myself a drink. When I return, he's still there, staring at the same spot on the floral wallpaper.

Time to get something on the table. "Did you... do you have an interest in Simona?"

His expression is unreadable when his cold, slate eyes drop to mine. The silence is brittle as ice.

I won't blink. "Seems like it would be better if we knew where you and I stand on this. Not that I plan on giving her up. You'll have a fight on your hands."

He runs a finger along the inside the collar of his t-shirt. "Sprite—she's a badass. What man like me wouldn't be attracted to that? Of course I think she's hot. But I'm damaged goods. The kind no woman wants to deal with."

I slosh my drink around and watch the gold liquid come dangerously close to the edge. "I feel ya, brother. That's why it surprises the hell out of me that she's down with... whatever this is."

"You're good for each other."

Tossing back the whiskey, I contemplate that. "Let's hope so, I'm just thankful she's in one piece."

"I second that. Now, how are we going to keep her that way?"

I scrub my hands over my face. "First things first, we need to figure out who put the reward out for her."

"Dickhead's digging around to find out about the other two people with bounties. I say we grab one of them and use them as bait." Andre pushes his empty glass across the coffee table and rises. He stretches, yawns like a big bear.

I'm nodding as a big ass grin spreads on my face. "I like the way you think, you big, bad mother fucker."

# CHAPTER TWENTY-SEVEN

## Simona

It's chaos in the sitting room when I walk out. I heard noises, but I had NO idea this is what was happening. Oh jeepers.

The room is filled with... all of the Agile Security and Rescue Team. Cole, Sierra, Roark, Mako, Andre, and Scotch.

In the center of the hive is a coffee table covered with French breakfast food in every conceivable form.

Looks like a party that I didn't get invited to. "What the hell is going on here?"

"Eating. Talking. Waiting for the princess to wake up," replies Cole with a big sarcastic grin on his face as he walks by.

Scotch's eyes follow me as I cross the room. I bump him with my shoulder when I pass. "Hey, you."

# CHAPTER 27

His expression softens but still feels distant as he lays his muscular arm around my shoulders.

"What are all of these crazies doing here?"

"Besides eating everything in sight?"

I grin. "Well, that's par for the course."

"They came to help."

Even though I knew that's why they were here, I'm still dumbfounded. "But this isn't a paying case."

Marshall steps into the room from Andre's half of the suite. He's hanging up a phone call as he walks in. An expression of relief softens his hard eyes. "Simona. Damn, woman, it's good to see you. I was beginning to wonder if the doctor there was lying about you being in that bedroom. You slept half the day away."

I cut my eyes to Scotch. "Someone didn't wake me up. When did you get here?"

"Landed just a couple of hours ago. Came as soon as we could."

"You shouldn't—"

The boss man cuts me a look that leaves no mistake—this is not open for discussion.

"Ugh. You guys." I throw up my hands and march to the center of the room. "There's nothing that warrants all of you being here. Please, don't pass up on paying gigs for this. Go home. After breakfast, of course, but I could never afford the team."

Marshall crosses his big arms as half his brow angles up. Oh no. I've seen that look. Mules are less stubborn than my boss when he hits no-can-do mode.

"Last I remembered, I was the one in charge. So, leave that for me to decide."

I shake my head as I massage my aching temple. "I'm at a loss for what to say."

Mako chuckles. "Well, that's a first."

I give the former SEAL a death glare.

Sierra, sitting next to her husband on the couch, kicks Mako in the shin with her leather boot. "Watch it, buddy. I know your weakness."

He leans in and grins, his all-American-boy face lighting up. "You do?"

"Broccoli. You cross me and I'll make sure it's in every take-out meal I'm responsible for until I'm good and satisfied."

Mako's smile disappears. "You wouldn't."

"Oh, but I would."

Andre chuckles as he inspects a mint green macaron. "Don't put it past her."

Knowing I have no choice but to give in to the madness, I drop down onto the floor, cross my legs and pluck a giant croissant from the pile of amazing looking baked stuff. "Someone did a fine job of getting breakfast. So, as they say, if you can't beat them, you might as well join them..."

By the end of the breakfast discussion, I know a little more, but not much more than I did last night. The team needed some social time, it seems. But I did learn that Pavel ended up at the hospital last night, but Andre promises me it's nothing serious.

*Yeah.* That worries me. He didn't take dragging me around on a wild goose chase on rutted third world roads after surgery seriously either. Andre's a tough case. 'Serious' could mean a lot of things. Painful, ugly things.

With a punch to his leg, I catch Marshall's attention. "Do we know exactly which forum or job board, whatever the hell place on the dark web that Pavel found the job on?"

"It's called BloodWork, one word."

I scrunch up my nose. "Ick. That's just sick to begin with."

"Yeah, we could get a lot of security and rescue work off of it, actually."

Scotch says, "Interesting. You mean look for people who've been targeted and then help them evade capture?"

"Yep. That and work with the authorities to bring down the person hiring and hopefully eliminate some of the sick fucks who are taking the jobs to begin."

This idea really resonates with me. "Well, if anything good comes out of this, then that makes me feel better. So, what's next?"

Marshall sets his coffee cup aside and flips open his notepad. "Simona, I think you should start digging around for a digital trail, reach out to Pavel to see what else he's learned. And of course, see what you can recall from your past that might have led to this. Andre is on guard duty for you."

I groan. "Come on. I'm fine. It's not like I can't take care of myself."

Scotch leans in and wraps me up in a hug. "Not for you to decide."

I huff out a breath as Marshall goes on with his list. "Scotch, you dig around with her and see if you can figure out what's triggered this bounty for our little Sprite. Roark, Cole and Sierra, you're with me. We're still working the kidnapping case for the little girl. We've got more to sort through. Mako, don't you already have a dark web avatar or persona or whatever the hell you use there?

"Yep."

"I want you to start looking for a way in on that forum."

Mako's eyes spark with the challenge. "I've already got some street cred with my avatar, which will help get me in."

Marshall slaps his notepad on the table. "Alright, that's it, people. It's a wrap. We'll reconvene whenever and wherever the next thing turns up. In the meantime, everyone watch your six. We've had enough blood loss for a long time."

# CHAPTER TWENTY-EIGHT

## Simona

The bedroom is quiet when I shut the door. Almost everyone's gone, so I decide to take advantage of Scotch and Andre talking in the living room. I've been dying to call Josef. Maybe he's got ideas or connections that can help me sort this nightmare out.

The phone rings a few times, then he pics up. "Child. How is Sweden?"

"I'm not there now. But just as I suspected, there's much more to see. I could use a tour guide, I suspect. Sweden is a very big place." Of course he knows I'm not in Sweden, but I keep it light in case someone is listening, even though we're on two new phones.

"How can I help?"

"Do you know much about the places I've been before, when I was a little kid?"

"Ah, you mean when you were still with your mother?"

"Yes."

"I don't know much, but I have something that might help."

My stomach clenches. For a few seconds, my mind fills with memories from those horrible times. "What's that?"

"Do you remember the old book you brought here once? It was wet and tattered and had belonged to your mother."

"Oh my god. I remember a little book being in the bottom of my duffel a million years ago. I never even looked at it." That was the last thing I had on my mind when I was on the street. Stealing and hiding to survive.

"Well, child, it was not just a book, it was a book of poems that had been used as a diary as well. And I have it. It took much work, but it dried enough to read. Which I promise you I did not do. But I thought if one day... one day, if you asked about that time, I'd share it with you."

My throat is tight with dread as I even consider looking at something that belonged to the woman who gave birth to me. "I'm stunned."

"Let's meet for lunch in a few days. I'll call you with details later."

"I'll be waiting."

"Be safe, child."

"You too, friend. And thank you. For thinking of that. You've been so kind to me."

"I look forward to seeing you."

# CHAPTER TWENTY-NINE

*Scotch*

I find Simona sitting cross legged in the middle of the bed, facing the window. "You alright?"

She glances slowly over her shoulder. "I'm okay. I just called a friend."

I ease down on the bed, cross my feet at the ankles and fall back. "You seem upset. Not that it's surprising, this is a lot to have over your head."

Her eyes fall to her twisting hands. "You read me too easily."

"What's up, sweetheart?"

"I've been thinking about what Pavel said. Over and over, of course. The part about me carrying some man's mark. Well, obviously, I know it wasn't my father. He's dead. I saw his body in the church during his funeral."

She turns to face me. "So, I called Josef, the man who

helped me when I was young. He knew my hometown, so I thought maybe he might know something. We're going to meet for lunch in a few days."

"That's good, babe. I think that's a great place to start."

She worries at her lower lip. Takes a steep breath. "Josef has a diary that belonged to my mother. One I've never read."

"And you think that could be relevant?"

She nods. "I didn't tell you this before, but one of the last things she ever said to me was that she hated me. That giving birth to me ruined her life."

My gut instantly ignites with rage. A thousand fire ants sting at my stomach. I'm up off the bed a second later. "Fucking cruel. No child should hear that."

"I did. It can't be taken back. But that's not what's important. I just have this feeling that maybe this birthmark has something to do with her hate for me."

She hops off the bed and strides to the window. "Everything with my parents is such a disastrous blackhole in my memory."

Flexing my hands, I fight the urge to go to her, but she's bristling with energy that says 'don't'. "I can see why."

She draws a finger down the cold glass pane of the window. "Their relationship was horrible. That's all I remember."

"Why do you think she'd say giving birth to you ruined her life?"

She shakes her head. "I can't figure it out, exactly."

I step up to her side, pushing my hands in my pockets. "You know postpartum depression changes some people. Permanently. And relationships aren't the same once a child is in the picture."

She sighs. "I know. Maybe it's why they both hated me."

## CHAPTER 29

I can't hold back any longer. I pull her into my arms with so much force she cries out. "I want to take it all away. I'd do it if I could."

She shakes her head against my chest. "No. It made me who I am."

My heart thuds and twists as I listen to her breathing. She's so fucking strong. I can't imagine what she's gone through. It's no wonder she's so defensive.

No wonder she was repulsed at my flirtation when she came into the clinic that night. Now I know. Trust comes really fucking hard for her.

And we're nowhere near done with the bastard who's hunting her.

"We'll get to the bottom of this."

"I need to go to Czech in a few days."

I turn her to me so I can see her eyes. "Just tell me when. I'm going too."

With a little eye roll, she says. "I figured as much. You're kind of hard to shake."

## CHAPTER THIRTY

## Sım⊕na

Snow covers the rolling hills and tall evergreens for miles around the tiny village. Scotch pulls the car into the lot next to the café on the edge of town. I can't help but admire the broad cut of his shoulders beneath the wool pea coat he has on as he walks around the car to open my door.

It's a pleasant momentary distraction from the nerves I've got in my belly.

Andre steps out of his own rented car and shrugs on a heavy leather coat. He doesn't make eye contact as he turns and walks away toward the café that Scotch and I are going to as well.

An electronic chime sounds when we walk in. A young woman greets us in Czech, "Dobrý den, vítejte"

"We're meeting that gentleman," I reply in my native tongue as I motion toward Josef in the back corner of the

## CHAPTER 30

restaurant. I'm so excited I want to run past her. It's been too long since I've seen my father figure.

Taking her time, the hostess escorts us through the narrow cafe to the back. Scotch walks close, his hand on my back the entire time.

Josef rises from his seat. The affection in his face makes tears sting my throat as he folds me in a hug. His voice is warm and just like it always has been as he says, "Ah, it's so good to see you."

I'm all chokey when I speak. "You too. It's been too long."

When he lets me go, I step back and give him a good look. "You look good."

He smiles softly. "You too, child. You are radiant today. I checked for bugs by the way."

I laugh appreciatively as he holds my hands for a few seconds longer. "Of course you did."

Josef turns his attention fully to my companion. "And who is your friend?"

"This is Dr. Jameson Scott."

Josef's wise gaze sizes up Scotch as they shake. "So, I heard you saved my favorite little hellion."

Scotch's smile tips up on one side. "I did. But I heard you did it first. Pleasure to meet you, Mr. Novotny."

My heart grows and heats up like the summer sun coming over the horizon. Glowing. So bright and warm.

I almost can't take it.

Having these two men together does something to my nerves. It warms me and makes me nervous in equal parts.

For some reason, it feels really, really important that they like each other. "You two, let's sit down, please."

Scotch holds out my chair. I catch the man who saved

me when I was just a teen watching as he takes his own seat across from us.

I shrug off my down jacket and scarf with Scotch's help. "I hope we didn't keep you long."

"I've only been here a few minutes. You were right on time."

The waitress comes to take our order. Since we just arrived and I don't know the menu, I suggest Josef order for us. Looking down his nose through his reading glasses, he considers the selections for a minute.

Scotch reaches for my hand under the table. My fingers are like ice and he folds them into his warm palm. The heat from him chases some of my worry away.

The thought of seeing my mother's journal is hanging over my head like a cloud that's ready to cover everything in ice.

When Josef's finished ordering lunch and the waitress is gone, he engages Scotch in his barely accented English. "Dr. Scott. I'm quite surprised you won the trust of this one."

Scotch squeezes my hand. With complete honesty on his handsome face, he says, "It wasn't easy. And to tell you the truth, I'm not sure I have, completely."

His words strike a chord in my heart. He's so damn perceptive.

It's true. I'm not sure I have let go of all the roadblocks to my trust. It's a long hard road, one I don't even have the map to.

Josef drinks from his coffee as he studies us together. "I can't say she's been fond of medical people since I met her. That makes this even more interesting."

I huff. "You would be mistrusting too if you had a mother that preached that doctors were the root of all evil."

## CHAPTER 30

Beside me, I feel a slight change in Scotch's body. A tensing of his muscles. A shift in his warmth. "It's understandable. It can be hard to trust if a doctor has hurt you or your family."

When his eyes turn to me, I know he's thinking about something. And I wonder if it's the same thing that's starting to unfurl in my head.

Did my mother's hate of doctors have something to do with her hate for me?

Shaking myself out of the rabbit hole, I turn my attention back to my dear friend. "Have you thought of anything which might help me figure this problem out?"

"I did a little asking around about you."

"Did anything new show up?"

"I actually know a woman that knew your mother when you were a very young child."

The clenching in my gut is getting tighter by the minute. Soon, it's going to choke the life out of me. "Yes, did she remember something important?"

"Your mother was quite different before you were born." He reaches into a leather sling bag hanging on the chair next to him. "This might help. I haven't read any of it. It's for you to decide if you want to."

My hand is numb and shaky as I reach across the table for the small hardbound book. It's dingy and stained. The edge of the cover is creased. The cover is embossed with a flaked off gold title that reads, malé básně. Translated to English, it's Little Poems.

Intentionally not reading anything inside, I thumb through the pages. "Why would anyone use this as a diary?"

Josef grins. "Little spy, think about that."

Scotch taps the book, "Because no one would think of it

being a journal. Just an old forgotten book sitting on the shelf."

Josef's grin is appreciative. "Smart man."

I stuff the small book in my coat pocket, unable to look at it any longer. Digging into that won't happen until I'm behind closed doors, alone.

"Is that your man over there?" Josef tips his head slightly toward Andre.

Scotch raises a brow. "Maybe."

Josef laughs. "He's discreet. I'm just wise."

"I have no doubt, Simona's very talented, and I heard she learned from the best."

The waitress approaches with our order. As she's passing out our plates Josef lightly comments, "He's smooth, I see why you like him."

I grumble as I take my plate. "Let's just say he's trouble."

The waitress scurries off and I see her chatting up Andre with a flirty grin on her face. I bet she does like the big American. He's not like your average Czech man. Andre's got this air of danger that surrounds him like a cloak.

I turn the conversation back to the bounty for my 'recovery.'

"I've dug through everything I can think of and nothing makes sense about this person who's looking for me. The two other people that are being hunted have similar characteristics as me, one with a similar birthmark."

Scotch rubs his hand over my thigh in a supportive gesture.

I take a breath and say what I've mentioned only to Scotch. "I think the others could be siblings that I don't know about."

## CHAPTER 30

Josef chews a bite of his *grilované klobásy*, and when he finishes, he says, "I think you're onto something, Simona."

"But who is our father?" I ask, knowing that none of us has the answer.

Scotch sets aside his fork. "Do you know who your mother's doctor was?"

I can't breathe for a minute. "I don't."

Josef takes a blank card from his sports coat pocket. He jots a name on the back and slides it across the table to Scotch. "This man knew him before he died."

That's not what I expected. "Oh..."

Josef's expression turns dark. "The doctor who delivered you died a short time ago. Not in a pretty way. And I heard that he was very frightened for some time before he met his demise. I thought you might want to know."

I let that news sink in as I push my food around. "I should speak to this man who knew the doctor."

Josef continues to eat. When he's done, he says, "Be careful, child. I understand you're on fire to dig this out, just don't lose your head."

Scotch wraps a possessive arm around my shoulder. "I'm not going to leave her side."

That seems to please Josef. The rest of the meal, we talk about the garden he raised in the summer. The forecast for more snow this weekend, and his interest in doing some travel when the weather breaks.

It's hard for me to follow along at first because my mind is full of details that don't add up, but I remind myself— You never know when the last chance to visit this man will be.

*So be present.* Be here.

With two men who've saved my life and given me support in my toughest hours.

We share laughs and finish our meal. And it soothes my heart. After long hugs in the cold air outside the restaurant, I say goodbye to Josef. "I'll call soon."

"Do. I will keep researching for your next trip."

"I can't thank you enough. For everything."

He ruffles my hair. "It's my pleasure. As it always has been."

I turn for the car and Josef calls Scotch back. Josef purposefully turns his back toward me. The sneaky devil. Of course he would make it so I can't see their faces. He knows I can read lips.

After a couple of minutes, they shake hands. Scotch ambles in his long-legged stride to the car, his expression surprisingly neutral.

The instant he's in the car, I'm drilling him. "What did he say?"

That wicked grin of his finally shows up. "Man talk."

I slip my hand under his coat and pinch the skin over his ribs as he backs out of the parking spot.

"Ouch."

"Seriously, I'd love to know what he said."

Scotch reaches for my hand. "He told me to keep a careful eye on you, that you're an expert at getting away from people. And... that he's counting on me to keep you close."

I grit my teeth. "He didn't."

He chuckles and looks at me for a second before he turns back to the road. "He did. And I told him he's right. And that I won't be making that mistake again."

I sag into the seat. "Great. Just what I need. Two of you ganging up on me."

"Three. Don't forget Andre."

I smack my forehead. "Crap."

"And Marshall. Cole. Mako. Sierra. Roark."

"I'm doomed. I had no idea what I was getting myself into when I signed on with Agile."

He laughs. Lifts my hand to his lips and brushes a kiss across my knuckles. "Neither did I. But as far as I'm concerned, I won the prize."

## CHAPTER THIRTY-ONE

# Sim⊕na

The night is almost as black as my short-bobbed wig. It's a perfect evening for a visit to Doctor Wilhelm Ostep's home.

The lights in his study glow warm, casting rectangles on the lawn outside of his house. Carefully, I maneuver around rose bushes that have been cut low for winter and peer in the window. He's sound asleep. Book on his lap, cat curled by his side on the loveseat.

It takes less than four seconds to pick the pathetic lock on his front door. Carefully, I close and lock it behind myself.

Ten minutes later, when Ostep wakes up, he blinks and sucks in a sharp breath.

"I'm not here to hurt you," I tell him in Czech.

He smooths his sweater and lifts the cat onto his lap. "Rather unusual way to call upon someone."

# CHAPTER 31

I adjust the fake glasses on my nose. "I'm a rather unusual guest."

"Indeed. Would you like some scotch?"

I twist my lips, "No. I don't like scotch." Total lie, of course. But my kind of Scotch is tall and strong and has a five o'clock shadow that I love on my clit.

"What can I do for you, my dear?"

"I have questions about your former coworker, Doctor Horak."

He frowns. "Many of us had questions about him."

"Do you know anything about his work with women and babies?"

The man glances down, watches his gnarled hands as he smoothes them over the cat's fur. "Ulrich, he told me once, many years ago, that he made his fortune off of helping someone have babies."

Something inside of me stills. Heavy, uncomfortable silence settles into the space between us.

"I'm not sure what you mean."

"Neither am I."

"My mother wrote in her diary that her doctor betrayed her. The last day I ever saw her, she said she hated me, hated giving birth to me. That I destroyed her life."

He watches me, his ancient eyes sharp on me as I continue, "It took some digging to figure out who her doctor was. But he's dead and I want answers."

"I see." He leans forward. "Come closer, my child. Let me see you."

Instead, I lean farther back. "That's of no importance."

"It could be. What color is your hair?"

"Black."

"Your wig is a lovely shade, my dear, but what color is your real hair?"

I chew my lip for a second. Terribly torn. "Blonde. I was born white blonde."

"And your parents are darkly complected?"

"They were. They're both dead. Why does that matter?"

"Something happened years ago. Something amiss that destroyed many families. Blonde children being born, out of turn."

He pauses and closes his eyes for a moment. "The myth was that eight children had been born within two years with striking stories. Stories of unplanned pregnancy. No similarity to parents or siblings. All had been born to patients of Horak."

I'm stunned so badly I wobble and sit down on the ottoman to keep from sinking to the floor.

"It's nothing more than a myth as far as I know."

I can't force my throat to work, to swallow down the horrible taste in my mouth. I'm frozen as my blood moves weakly through veins made of ice.

The doorbell startles us both.

He glances toward the front of the house. "I'm sorry, but you'll have to excuse me. That's my lady coming over for a late-night visit. You'll have to leave by the back. I wouldn't want her to think I had another caller."

Numbly, I rise off the ottoman and follow him toward the rear of the house.

"Good luck, miss. I hope you find the answers you seek. But a word of caution. Be careful who you ask. Horak's death was not an accident."

"It would be best if you tell no one of my visit."

"But of course, a gentleman never mentions his callers."

I step into the black night, tip my head in thanks, and disappear.

## CHAPTER THIRTY-TWO

*Scotch*

The pulse in Simona's neck is jumping wildly when she slips into the car.

"Shit," she mutters as she rolls down the window.

"Ready to get out of here?"

She rips off the wig. "Yeah. Go."

I pull onto the road. Far behind me, Andre's lights come on. I reach for her. "What happened? I was watching you with the binoculars, but obviously something happened that upset you."

"I just need some air. I feel kind of dizzy."

Glancing at her, I see her color is off. "Lean your seat back. Get your breathing under control."

She instantly complies which tells me how off she must feel. No fight at all. That's a warning flag for sure. "Talk to me."

"I'm a little out of breath right now."

Using navigation, I follow the route across town toward the highway. "Do you need to pull over?"

"Yes. Yes. Please—"

She's out of the car on the side of the road before I can get the car in park. Andre passes us slowly. I know he'll stop nearby.

"Babe, what the hell is going on?"

"I just needed some air."

I grab her arm. "Whoa. Hold still. Let me look at you."

She huffs. "I'm fine."

"You're pale."

Pulling against my hold, she growls at me, "I'm freaking upset."

"I can see that. Now, what happened?"

"He told me that there were eight kids born around the same time as me that were not what their parents expected."

My brain can't quite grasp what she's saying. "Eight infants born that were not expected? That happens a lot. Accidental pregnancy."

She twists out of my hand. "No, Scotch. Something different. He knew I was blonde and that my parents weren't."

Pacing, she jams her hands in her hair. Then she stops and glances at me... Right before she falls like a tree, in a dead faint.

Fuck!

My heart nearly stops. I'm on her a second later. She's coming around. Gravel is stuck to the side of her face. I brush it off. "Damnit. Simona, have you always been a fainter?"

She frowns. "No." Looking around, she says, "Oh no. It happened again."

## CHAPTER 32

"Just lay there. Don't move."

She pushes up on her elbows. I ease her back down.

"We need to get you to a hospital."

"I'm fine. I fainted. It's not the end of the world."

Unconvinced, I say, "You're not winning this argument."

Bristling mad, she won't look at me the whole way to the hospital.

I could give a damn. I'm only worried about her and nothing will keep me from taking care of her.

## CHAPTER THIRTY-THREE

## Sim⊕na

"Simona Novotny."

I toss the five-year-old fashion magazine aside. "Yes."

The nurse that I haven't seen before smiles. "You're pregnant."

My mouth drops open but nothing comes out.

Obviously used to seeing women with my expression and soundless gaping pie holes, she says, "Okay, now that you know what has caused your fainting, you must visit your doctor immediately."

"*What?* Huh?"

"Your doctor. Schedule a visit right away to begin prenatal care."

A choked sound comes from my throat. "Wait. I have a thing."

Her very manicured brow raises. "A thing? *A penis?* Yes, that's how most pregnancies happen."

## CHAPTER 33

"No! An implant."

"*Oh*, birth control. It didn't work. See your doctor immediately."

She jerks the sheet off of me. "I'll bring your husband in to walk you out."

# CHAPTER THIRTY-FOUR

*Scotch*

Simona waves a hand at me when I ask about what the doctor said. "It's nothing."

Planting my feet, I give her what should be a wilting look. "I'm not moving until I know what's up."

Simona slides off the bed ignoring me. "It's nothing."

I catch her arm to make sure she's steady. "We're not leaving here until I know what's up."

"I fainted, *Doctor*. You know what's up."

I growl, "Get back in that bed."

"They released me."

I back her up, step by step until the backs of her legs bump the bed. "Sit."

Snarling at me, she sits on the edge of the bed.

"Do. Not. Move."

She sighs. I turn and stomp toward the nurses' station.

## CHAPTER 34

A young nurse dressed in green scrubs smiles. "Ah, Mr. Novotny. Can I help you?"

"Yes, and actually, it's Doctor. I'd like to get some details on my... wife's blood tests."

She grins and glances at my junk. "She's got the results." She pivots on her heels and swaggers off, disappearing into another patient's room.

What the hell?

I storm back into Simona's room, as I round the corner I'm muttering. "Well, that went really well—"

My feet freeze in their tracks. "Simona?"

The room is empty.

# CHAPTER THIRTY-FIVE

*Scotch*

I'm so mad I could spit nails through the side of a car. "How the hell did she get away from us?"

Andre eyes me as if this is all my fault.

Gritting my teeth, I say, "I didn't do anything."

"She obviously didn't want to see you."

"Look, I don't know anything about what happened in there before I walked in. All I know is that I wanted her to tell me. She wouldn't, so I asked the nurse to tell me."

Andre raises a brow. "That's doing something."

I shake my head and press at the spot where I'm sure there is an icepick sticking out of my skull. "That's nothing new. She knew I was going to be involved. I mean, Christ. I am a doctor."

Sighing, Andre climbs into his rented car. "Maybe there was something she didn't want you to know."

## CHAPTER 35

I turn to a sudden block of ice.

He shuts the door and starts the engine as I stare at him going over a million possibilities. "I'm going to look for her. You might want to as well." He puts the car in reverse and backs out.

"Fuck," I growl and stomp toward the car Simona and I arrived in together. She did it again.

## CHAPTER THIRTY-SIX

## Sim⊕na

The little cabin is exactly as I remember it. Tucked into the mountainside, draped in heavy green boughs and dollops of snow. Josef never put a real lock on the door, so I'm inside in a few seconds, even without my lock pick set.

The interior is dark and cold, and perfectly quiet. Just as I knew it would be. The perfect place to hole up as I try to hang on to the tiny remaining threads of my sanity.

This place always brought me peace. I just hope it can now. Because there's a tornado of emotion inside of me and I don't have a root cellar to hide in.

Moving to the fireplace, I use the supplies he always has on hand to start a roaring fire. The paper and tinder glow and crack. Fire spreads to the logs before long and the cabin begins to warm.

Red, yellow, and even blue flames dance as I lose myself in the mesmerizing sway of the colors.

## CHAPTER 36

Pregnant.

Me. Of all people. Now. Of all times. With Scotch, my rescuer, my coworker, my hopeless addiction.

But the crazy thing between us is just that. Crazy.

And I, Simona Novotny, an orphaned spy who lives life by the seat of her tactical pants, has NO idea how to be a mother.

I can't even take care of a plant.

How does someone who's never had roots give roots to a child?

A little bitty, tiny little baby human that needs human baby things.

Lots of things.

Like a warm safe place.

And food.

And love.

My heart squeezes and flips itself inside out. Love.

I suck at love. If I didn't get the hives every time I think about the concept, I wouldn't be here right now. I'd be facing the man who so handily supplied the sperm which created our child. I'd be telling him how happy I am. How much I love the idea of having a family with him.

But no. Here I am. Hiding. Running. Unsure of everything.

How do you love a baby when you didn't even know what love was? Not like I have a lot of friends to emulate. Hell, the only person I even know who's been pregnant is Sierra.

Tears spring to my eyes. *Oh god.* Sierra is amazing.

I'm nothing like her. We're from different planets.

And Scotch... Well, he's a lot of things, but he's nothing like Cole or the Strong brothers. They have roots. And I can't see Scotch chasing the standard American dream—house, wife, kids & dog.

If he was, he'd have done that a long time ago.

Nope, we're nothing like those people. We're birds of a feather. Wandering on curiosity and adrenaline.

The tears come. And come. And come. *God.*

*How will I tell him?*

He trusted me. I told him I had an implant.

If I were in his shoes, I'd be furious.

Swiping at my tears, I fight the wave of guilt and uncertainty that is clawing at my lungs. I have to tell him. I just don't know how.

The weight of responsibility is so heavy it nearly crushes me into the hundred-year-old wooden flooring.

I don't know what to do for the first time since I was thirteen.

When I walked out that door of the school the day my mother died, I knew it was me for me.

That was it. No one else. Nothing else mattered.

I had to eat. I had to survive, no matter how many crimes or what terrible things I had to do.

And now... now this little tiny baby is going to depend on me.

Scotch is going to expect things from me. Even if it's just to share custody or do whatever people who have babies together do.

All of it is a great big fat yawning black hole of unknowns.

Wrapping my arms around myself, I pray for guidance. "I could use some help down here. If there is a god, or goddess, or whatever, I need a pick-me up right about now because my already screwed up life just got really crazy."

Fear suddenly lances through my body. I leap from the

floor and rush to the little bathroom. Yes. It's still there! I snatch the first aid kit off the shelf.

Pressing my hand to my stomach, I whisper, "Hang on, little one. I'll get this thing out of my arm so there's no way it can harm you."

By the time I return, the fire's burning low. Soon, I'll need to stoke it to keep warm. Outside, the wind is whistling against the eaves of the cabin as the night turns to the darkest, coldest hours of night.

I curl deeper into the wool blankets on the couch. Numb. Sad. Confused. Tomorrow, I need to make some calls. But tonight, I need sleep.

## CHAPTER THIRTY-SEVEN

*Scotch*

The old truck's headlights shine through a barrage of snowflakes. It's cold as hell. The heater on the old truck is barely able to keep the temp above fifty in the cab. For the last half hour, the thing's tires have crunched along a road through the forest that's covered in a thick layer of snow.

"She's here," Josef assures me. "Like I mentioned, she tripped my new security system." He grins. "I got one over on her this time. A fancy new LIDAR system with remote cameras that follow the detected person. Quite slick. She got here at twelve thirty-one."

"So, she came straight here from the hospital. But how?"

"Probably hitchhiked since I haven't seen any stolen vehicles discarded along the way."

The idea of her hitchhiking nearly makes my head explode.

## CHAPTER 37

For the tenth time tonight.

Thank fuck I found Josef.

Well, actually, Andre found Josef, thanks to the curvy brunette in the cafe. He sweet-talked her right out of the intel we needed.

She knew which area of town he lived in. From there it only took a little snooping around to find the car that Andre saw him leave the cafe in. It was tucked in a garage next to the truck we are in now.

"Simona aged me twenty years tonight," I mutter as I pull my coat collar tighter. It's not just the cold in the truck that's making me cold. It's the clawing terror in my gut. "At first, I thought someone grabbed her. But security at the hospital made it plain and clear no such thing would happen at their facility. And they backed that up by showing me a security camera screenshot of Simona sprinting across the parking lot. Alone."

"I warned you. She's slippery," he says with a warm chuckle.

"Slippery is fine. But I'm confused as hell about what would send her scrambling," I motion toward the forest on either side of the road, "into the damned wilderness in the dark."

As we putt along on the narrow lane, he says, "Simona likes to come here when she's confused or mad."

I run my hands through my hair for the hundredth time. "Do you think she's trying to pull some crazy shit like going vigilante on whoever this is that's got a ransom out for her?"

Josef shrugs. "Always a possibility, but that's not my first guess."

Chewing a hole through the inside of my cheek, I curse how slow he's going. "What is your first guess?"

His eyes crinkle as he grins. "I'd say it's you."

"Me?" I stare at him.

"Just a hunch."

I shake my head. "She's..."

"Challenging?"

Pressing on my eyeball, I reply. "Confusing."

We putter along for another few minutes. "I'll admit, I'm pretty fucking jacked right now. All I can think is she must have gotten bad news. Why else would she run?"

"She's healthy as a horse. That girl's never been sick."

I grumble. "Well, fainting is plenty of a reason for me to be worried."

Josef glances at me. "Is it?"

"Damned right it is."

He goes back to carefully watching the road. After forever, we come to a stop, deep in the forest. "It's up there. Take the path. Follow the smoke from the chimney." He tosses me a flashlight and a burner phone. "Call me if you need provisions. My number's programmed in. There's enough food, water, and wood to last a couple of days. There's a snowmobile in the shed."

As soon as I jump from the truck, he's backing up and turning around. The dim tail lights of the old truck quickly disappear into the heavy falling snow.

Exactly seven minutes later, I'm knocking on the door of a tiny, rustic cabin, praying I don't get shot and disposed of in the snowbank I just trudged through. "Simona..."

Footsteps make the floor creak behind the heavy wooden door. I realize I may have miscalculated. Maybe the element of surprise would have been better. But I haven't picked a single lock in my life.

I've kicked down a few doors, but somehow that just seems wrong. It is Joseph's cabin. And she is safe inside of it.

## CHAPTER 37

Fighting to keep a growl out of my voice, I call to her. "Simona, open up."

The latch clicks. When the door swings wide, I'm met with the muzzle of a very big shotgun. I sigh in relief. Never has a gun pointing in my direction looked so good.

"Sprite. Damn, I'm glad to see you."

Simona's eyes are brimming with tears. Her throat works. "You found me."

I push the gun aside and jerk her to me. "Damn right I found you. Again," I murmur against her hair. "You might as well give up. I'm stubborn. I'm mad too, which makes me even more determined."

She leans down and sets the shotgun on the floor. Tentatively, she wraps her arms around my neck. "I wasn't really going to shoot you."

"I know."

I steal her breath with a kiss that's barely restrained. I want to crush her sweet lips, ravish her with all the frustration I've got knotted up in me. But I don't.

She leans back. "Josef brought you?"

"Yes."

Squinching up her cute nose, she says, "That devil."

I grin as I rub a thumb across her cheek. Across the mark that's turned the world upside down. "I'm pretty sure he's an angel."

She drops her lashes. "Actually, I have to agree with you on that. How did he know I was here?"

I pull her against me, tighter. Feeling how damned perfect this infuriating woman fits in my arms. "That's for him to tell you."

Before she can get away, I swing her up into my arms and carry her to the couch. "Now, you *are* going to talk. Even if I have to handcuff myself to you."

She buries her head in my shoulder. "Scotch..."

And the tone of her voice makes all that fear inside of me unspool into a messy tangle. I fight the urge to snap as icy terror drops into my limbs. "What did the doctor tell you?"

# CHAPTER THIRTY-EIGHT

## Simona

He's here.

Him. The man who saved me. The one who rocked my world and tossed it upside down. The devil who won't stop pushing his way into every single aspect of my life.

Some part of my mind knew he'd find me. Just not so fast.

*I'm not ready.*

I've never been so scared in my life.

I've done crazy stuff. Broken into multimillion dollar corporations. Snuck into people's homes to plant cameras. Run from guard dogs. Stolen cars while people loaded the trunk with contraband. Dodged gun-toting maniacs. Taken a bullet at close range. Looked death in the eye.

But nothing has ever felt so damned scary as the two little words I need to say.

*Gah!*

I'm suddenly mute and sweating cold, angry bullets.

Scotch cradles my face in his big hands and kills me with the worry in his words. "Honey. You're scaring the fuck out of me, right now. Did something bad show up on the tests?"

I nod. Then I shake my head. Then I do that weird thing that some people do that's both a yes and no at the same time. Some kind of bobblehead mashup.

Then I burst into tears.

God! Is this what being pregnant is going to feel like? I'm not okay with this.

Those dark brows of Scotch's fall into a serious line as he holds me. "Just tell me. We'll figure it out together. I promise."

I open my mouth, but have to clear my throat. As my heart pounds, he says, "It's okay. It's *okay*, whatever it is."

Yeah, well, that might be about to change.

I cannot say those two words...

"I'm sorry. I just got... claustrophobic. This whole thing is making me crazy." That and finding out I have a little human growing inside of me. Lord. Help. Me.

And Scotch is having none of it. "What are you not telling me?"

I open my mouth a few times. But can't get it out. So, I do the best that I can. My voice comes out all shaky and weird. "Remember the implant I had in my arm?"

That frown of his grows harder. I slide my sleeve off my shoulder. There's a tiny round bandage over the hole where the birth-control implant used to be.

"What the *hell*?"

Nervously, I say, "I cut it out."

He's baffled. His eyes go wide, then hard. "You're certifiable. I mean, I could have taken it out. But what the hell did you do that for?"

"It failed."

Silence drops like a bomb between us.

That old saying about seeing someone's cogs turning... well, I'm watching it happen first hand.

He's going to short out that big brain of his.

"I'm p-p-pregnant."

For thirty seconds, I think I might faint again, from sheer gut-twisting, vein-popping anticipation.

"Say something," I blurt.

But he doesn't. He just looks at me. I mean, really looks at me. With every damned emotion a man can have in his dark brown irises.

He lifts a hand to my face again. Cups my jaw with his calloused fingers. "Don't ever, ever, be afraid to talk to me again. Promise me?"

I nod. Even though promising this to him is almost as scary as telling him I was pregnant just now.

And when I think I'm about to snap into a million pieces, he whispers, "I don't know what to say."

I nod because I'm too broken to speak.

"I'm not equipped to be a father." His concerned eyes bore into mine.

I flinch and pull away. I knew he'd feel this way. Hell, I feel this way. I'm not equipped to be anything to anyone else. I'm solo. Always and forever. Only, now that's all changed.

"I'm sorry," I whisper, my voice breaking.

He grabs my arm and turns me back around. His voice goes low. It's rusty and hard like an old hinge. "You're sorry?"

"I knew you'd be upset."

He shoves a hand into his thick hair. "I'm not upset. I'm in shock."

What?!? You?

"Well, how do you think I feel?"

He huffs out a breath as he drops his hands to his hips. "I can't imagine."

Throwing my own hands into the air, I half shout. "I don't know how to be a mother."

Forever, he just looks at me. Then his frown slowly turns to a grin. "Well, once upon a time I didn't know how to be a surgeon. And you didn't know how to be a badass spy girl. Guess we've got to figure it out."

"Are you crazy?"

"No more than you."

"Look, Scotch, I understand that you'd not be the settling down kind or whatever they say in America."

"Damn right I'm not. But I'm pretty sure you're not the settling down kind either."

I shake my head. "No. I'm not."

He takes a step toward me. "Well, more than one child has been raised in unconventional ways. I mean, look at you. You turned out perfect."

I blink and look away as tears make my lashes glisten in the firelight. "Perfect. I'm far from it."

He wraps me up from behind, pulling me against his thick chest. His lips are against my ear when he whispers. "Perfect for me. Perfect to be the mother of my child."

With my heart walking a tightrope, I ask what I'm dying to know, "You're happy about this?"

"Fuck, yes. I'm happy. I love the fact that you've got my seed growing inside of you. I never knew how I'd feel. But now I know. And I'm over the damned moon." He spreads his big palm over my stomach as his warmth surrounds me.

I fight to control the sobs that want to escape my chest. Fear. Joy. Overwhelm. It's all bottled up inside of me.

After a minute, he laughs as his scruff rubs against my cheek. "Man. Our world is about to get crazy."

As if it wasn't crazy enough already.

# CHAPTER THIRTY-NINE

*Scotch*

The fire is roaring again after I add some logs. "So, are we laying low here for a few days? Sounds like Josef's got the place stocked."

Simona shrugs and wraps a wool blanket more tightly around herself. "I don't know. I just sort of needed a place to get my head together."

She holds the blanket back for me, welcoming me, when I return to the couch. She's all soft, and warm, and snugly beneath, and all I can think about is keeping her naked for a few days. "I could see us staying here for a while."

Her little grin turns naughty. "That could be fun. I mean… if it's safe to have sex while I'm p-pregnant."

I laugh. "That is one thing I do know about pregnancy. It's all good. We can continue to have lots of fun."

## CHAPTER 39

Her relief is visible. "Whew. Okay, because I feel really aroused right now."

Growling, I lean over and nip at the cord of her neck. When I hear my phone ringing across the room, I curse. "Damn. I guess I should get that." After fishing my phone out of my coat pocket, I check the screen. "It's Marshall."

Simona perks up and slides to the end of the couch nearest me.

"Hey, man."

He cuts right through the chase, as usual. "Pavel got us on the tail of one of the two other people with bounties on them."

I hit the speaker button and lean a hip on the edge of the couch. "Go ahead. We're both here."

"The other jobs posted on BloodWork are for the return or collection of two people, as you know. One male. One female. We located the male. Mako's picking him up as we speak. He's going to have a sit down with you both."

Simona's fingers go to her mouth. "Where?"

"In Germany. Not that far from you. His name is Wolf Black. He's twenty-nine. Get this. He's in the SAS."

Nodding in appreciation, I say, "Well, he's probably able to take care of himself, at least."

Marshall chuckles. "He's definitely prepared for almost anything. Oh, and Andre is dropping off this because he's going to take a security detail for me. Since Scotch, Mako and this SAS guy are going to be with you, Simona, I thought it would be fine."

Simona's already off the couch. "Sure, understood. Just say where we need to be."

Marshall gives us the details and Simona confirms she knows exactly where we are going. Buzzing around the cabin, she makes preparations for us to leave. Putting things away, and smothering the fire. That's when I remember we don't have wheels. "How are we getting out of here?"

She glances at me over her shoulder. "Snowmobile, of course."

"Uh. Okay. Of course."

Laughing, she tosses me my coat. "Never been on one?"

"Nope. I guess this is a day of firsts. Never been an expecting father, never torn through the Czech countryside on a snowmobile. Who knows what's about to happen next."

* * *

Josef opens the door with a tight expression on his face. Looking over the top of his glasses, he says, "Well, at least you're together this time."

Simona steps into the foyer. I follow her into the tidy cottage. Josef's definitely eyeing me with suspicion as she hugs him. She says, "We can't stay. We have to go to Germany. Just picking up the rental car."

"Is everything okay?"

"The team found one of them."

He raises a brow. "That's good. This should help you figure out more."

"The snowmobile is in the garage," I say as I shake the older man's hand.

"I saw," he says with a grin. "Lots of surveillance experiments around here."

He turns to Simona, "Are you feeling alright, dear?"

"Oh. I am. Don't worry about me, please."

"I'm glad to see you two are working together again."

Simona glances at me as she nibbles her lip. "Me too."

He sees us off and I wonder when Simona will tell the

man about the pregnancy. I have a suspicion he'll be as excited as I am. But I could be wrong.

In the seat beside me on the way to Germany, Simona's intensely serious. I reach for her hand. The tips of her fingers are cool. "You okay?"

"I can't imagine who I'm about to meet."

"Don't overthink it."

She chuckles. "Impossible. I'm the queen of analyzing. Speaking of, did you see the way Josef was looking at us?"

I laugh. "Us? You mean looking at me like I'd done something to his baby girl?"

Her lips press together to cover her smile. "He kind of was looking at you like he might throw you into the cell in his basement."

I do a double take.

She bursts out laughing. "You should see your expression."

"That's another first I don't want to have today."

"Well, I think I'm getting the next mind-bender—Meeting someone who might be my brother."

## CHAPTER FORTY

## Simona

After crossing the border into Germany, it takes less than a half hour to reach the hotel where we are supposed to meet Mako and this stranger, Wolf Black.

But I swear the drive has never felt longer.

Scotch parks in the small lot next to the slender brick building. He catches me for a quick kiss. "You're going to wear a hole in your jeans if you keep rubbing your palms on your thighs."

"It's ridiculous, I know."

He opens my door and I hop from the car, eager to get on with this. Scotch catches up to me and grabs my hand, which he holds firmly as we cross the lot and enter the small lobby. As if I might try to get away again.

I can't help feeling squirrelly. I always took off when trouble reared up. That kept me safe and alive for all of my life.

## CHAPTER 40

The lobby is quiet. It's early morning and only the staff are around. No one looks twice when we take the stairs to the second floor. Scotch lightly knocks on the door to room 203.

I nearly chew my lip in half while we wait. Holy smokes. It feels like the twilight zone.

Mako's eyes have deep shadows under them when he opens the door. He motions us inside with a tilt of his head. "Come on in."

I draw a deep breath as I step around him. Here we go. Without hesitation, I stalk into the small hotel room.

Sitting on the foot of the bed at the far side of the room is a young, lean, dark blond man. When he turns to face me, I'm struck frozen like I've been locked inside a block of concrete.

This man is a male version of me.

Same high cheekbones. Same slender nose. Same arch to our brows. His hair is a few shades darker. But otherwise, we look damned close to the same.

He stands up. The man is tall. Way taller than me. He's muscular with a sharp, knowing gaze, the same color as mine. Slowly, he looks me over. His English is clear with just a slight hint of some undetermined Eastern European accent. "What the bloody hell?"

"Things just got weird," I reply roughly.

He shakes his head with his expression clearly one of disbelief. "Mother of god. It's like I'm looking in a mirror. Well, sort of. If I was a crossdressing little sprite of a thing. I heard you have the same birthmark."

"Geez. That was a mouthful. And apparently, we do have the same birthmark."

He turns his cheek toward me, taps his finger above the five o'clock shadow. I step closer for a look. There, in damn near the same spot as mine, is a mark that's so close to mine it's eerie. We both bear the same moon shaped birthmark without a doubt.

I can't hold back the "eeep" that forms in my throat.

I turn my face so he can see mine.

Curtly, he asks, "Does this prove we are siblings?"

Scotch moves to my side. "There's a strong probability you have very close genetic similarities if you carry a birthmark like that."

The man's voice edges harder. "My mother gave birth to me. She'd never cheat on my father. How does this happen?"

"Hell if I know." I move to the other bed and drop down to sit on the edge as I try to put together the pieces from my very faded memory. My years with my mother weren't exactly full of loving moments of sharing. It was as if she never wanted me.

"My mother supposedly delivered me too. Which makes me think they were inseminated with someone's sperm."

Wolf huffs out a breath as he sits on the edge of the other bed. Steepling his fingers, he says, "Yeah, our father's sperm. Whoever the son of a bitch is."

Scotch folds his arm as he leans a shoulder against the wall. "The only way to know will be a DNA test."

Sign me up. I want to know. Even though in my heart now, I can't deny that this man looks like a brother. "Where can we get one?"

"I'll make some calls and find out."

Wolf says, "Now onto the other bizarre part of this, I understand we are being hunted and the bounty is quite large."

I push my hair back. "Yes, gigantic, actually. Two mil.

And if it was above table, something honest, I think a private investigative firm would be doing the looking. Pavel, the man who was trying to capture me, he said it was for my return to someone who owns me."

When Wolf's face morphs into anger, I see so much of myself in him. "Owns you? That's unbelievable."

Mako tips his chin toward his laptop. "Pavel said that they are using the same language in the ad for returning you, Wolf. That he owns you."

Wolf's face reddens, and a vein lifts on his forehead. His laugh is short, dark, and dangerous-sounding as his fingers ball into fists. "If someone thinks they're going to capture me and force me into something I don't want, they have another thing coming. I'll rip their bloody limbs off."

This brightens my day. A whole lot.

I'm not the only one who feels this way. "I like you already. So, you've got skills?"

His eyes cut to mine. "I'm in the SAS. I do it all, bombs, guns, choppers, mountaineering, intel."

I tilt my head toward him, "I guess that's a start."

For the first time, he smiles. It's broad and genuine. And I feel my heart expand. *A brother.*

Wow, I never imagined something like this could happen.

The sensation is almost overwhelming.

"It's nice to meet you, Simona," he says, extending his hand.

I accept, but quickly find myself hugging his muscular torso. "I've just got this sensation that my life makes a whole lot more sense, even if it doesn't."

He ruffles my hair. "Yeah, I know what you mean. I'm nothing like my parents." He steps back and motions toward

Scotch. "Now, why don't you introduce me to your fellow there before he cuts me down with those murderous glares."

I laugh, "Oh! Yeah, him. He's a bit overprotective."

Scotch pushes off the wall. "I am. You would be too if she was your woman and was carrying your child."

I'm so flabbergasted that my mouth has to look like a fish gulping for water. "Scotch!" As my face heats, I say, "We haven't told anyone yet. We just found out."

Mako snorts and tries to cover his sound of disbelief with a cough.

Scotch pulls me to his side, extends his hand. "I'm Jameson Scott, call me Scotch if you want."

The man who looks so much like me replies, "Wolf Black. They call me Shadow."

"Nice to meet you, Shadow."

Wolf narrows his eyes as he gives Scotch a quick assessment once again. "I have to say, I'm glad my possible sister isn't weighed down with some pansy-ass no good slacker."

Scotch glances at me. "I think we'll get along just fine."

Wolf smiles again, this time it's more feral. "Let's figure out how the four of us are going to kick some ass."

# CHAPTER FORTY-ONE

*Scotch*

Over takeout food, we review all the details that have been gathered so far. Something has been bothering me. "Didn't that doctor tell you there were eight babies born unexpectedly?"

Simona nods as she picks crispy wonton up with her pair of chopsticks. "Yes." She shivers. "Weird. To think we could have six other maybe-siblings."

Wolf frowns. "I'll admit that idea is a bit overwhelming to me. I'm not too interested in meeting many more of myself."

"Me too. I just can't figure out what the motive of someone would be to make children they didn't raise."

Mako sips off a can of seltzer, then places it back on the table. "You know this sounds like we are dealing with a megalomaniac."

I chew a bit of my Pad Thai and consider that. "You know, you could be onto something there. There have been cases where doctors inseminated people with their own sperm because of the power trip. But if your doctor is dead now, then that doesn't make sense. Plus, would he really have six million dollars in rewards to offer?"

Wolf's brows knot together. "That kind of money means that the person behind this is seriously flush with cash."

Simona taps her chopstick against her plate as she thinks. "Now, why would we be so valuable to someone?"

I remind them, "The two of you have some unique skills."

She cuts her eyes my way. "But this person didn't know that when he fathered us."

Wolf grumbles. "But we could have been genetically designed to have certain characteristics."

"That's just gross." Simona pushes her plate away.

"Is it? I mean, natural mate selection works that way as well. Humans look for mates that give them an evolutionary advantage. It's just more subconscious."

Wolf scrubs his hand over his stubble. "I do have a lot of characteristics that make me good at what I do."

"Cocky much?" Simona says with a teasing grin.

"No, it's true. And you? I bet you've got a good memory, a propensity for technical things, speed, stamina, and agility. Am I right?"

"I guess you're right."

Wolf goes back to eating. After his next bite, he says, "And my birth parents were none of those things. My father was a gangly, tall, scientist, so he had the brains. And my mother is a lifelong housewife with the coordination of a toddler. Lovely lady, but she's not exactly SAS material."

Simona leans in and rests her elbow on the table. "Same

here. Which makes me really think that it wasn't my mother's egg."

"Ditto," says Wolf.

Simona rubs her eyes tiredly. "So, what are we then? What were we made for?"

I say, "That's a very good question. If some rich man wanted children with these characteristics, then he probably had something in mind. But, at the same time, those characteristics would just generally be considered traits for high likelihood of success in the world."

Mako chimes in, "He could have just wanted to model you after himself."

I drink from my bottle of water while I contemplate this. "For some reason, he didn't raise you, if that is indeed the case."

Wolf and Simona suddenly talk over one another.

"Go ahead," Wolf grins, motioning toward Simona with his chopsticks.

Simona is practically bouncing in her seat. "I know why! Diversity. He wanted us to have diverse experiences."

Mako casually says, "Sounds like he's building some kind of team."

"Exactly!" Simona chirps.

With a hard expression, Wolf glances at me. I know what he's thinking. I just say it out loud. "This can't be for anything good. It's all too dark and scheming."

Wolf says, "I think it's time for Mako here to claim the money and take me in for the exchange."

Simona's eyes narrow. "You're going to go as the decoy?"

He leans back in his chair and raises a brow. "I think this would work. And you're sure as hell not going."

The line of her mouth presses flat before she takes a defensive tone. "I didn't necessarily say I was."

He chuckles softly, "But you thought it, didn't you?"

Her frustration makes the color on her cheeks turn pinker. "Why would you say that?"

"Because I know what you think already."

Simona smacks her forehead. "Heaven help me. Not someone else telling me what I'm thinking or what to do. I don't know if I can take it."

Wolf and I share a glance. He grins when I say, "Thank you, maybe the two of us can make her understand that putting herself in danger isn't going to fly."

Now, if only I could figure out how to keep her away while the rest of this damned situation is figured out and taken care of once and for all.

## CHAPTER FORTY-TWO

# Simona

The bathroom tile is cold beneath my bare feet as I brush my teeth. Scotch steps into the small room behind me. His eyes hold mine in the mirror. I rinse and dab my mouth with the hand towel. "What's wrong?"

"I'll be glad when all this shit is done."

"Me too..."

He wraps his arms around me from behind. His palm spreads over my stomach. "Are you feeling any effects?"

"A little tired, maybe. My nipples were more tender today."

"I've got to study up on all of this."

I grimace. "Please don't talk about what's to come. I think I might freak out. Okay?"

He nods solemnly. "Promise me something."

Uh oh.

"What's that?"

"You won't put yourself in harm as we take this S.O.B. down. I want to send you away and lock you up somewhere, but I know you will only hate me for it. And I already have three strikes against me. Actually, maybe four."

I reach behind me and press my palm to his hard jaw. "Yeah, four strikes, huh?"

"Being a doctor. Being a man. Chasing you when you ran, twice."

"Oh... Those. Yes. But I'm thinking I could forgive most of them."

He nuzzles his nose against my cheek. "You like the man part."

I can't hide my giggle. "I do like your man parts."

"I knew you did. Little screamer."

My face instantly burns. "You do it to me."

His eyes fill with heat and pride. "I'm glad I get you off like that."

"Well, you should be proud. I swear, sometimes, I think I might die from ecstasy."

He skims his open mouth along my neck. "My sweet, sexy Simona, I want you..."

A little shiver races down my spine. "Mmmm. I like the sound of that."

His warm fingers slide below my sweater and skim along the top of my jeans. My body starts to undulate on its own as his fingers graze, and knead, and do delicious things to my skin.

Eyes closed, I drift into a blissful state of arousal. God, I love his touch.

"You haven't promised me what I asked you to yet."

My eyes flip open. He's staring right at me in the mirror. "That was evil. Low. Conniving."

He dips his hand down, presses the heel of his palm

against my mound. "All's fair in love and war, my dear. You know this."

I close my eyes again as pleasure overtakes me. The heat of his hand sears through my jeans and makes my pussy pulse with need. "Okay. I promise."

"Look at me. Say it while you look at me."

Opening my eyes again, I hold his gaze in our reflection. "I promise you I won't put myself in harm's way unless it's protecting the people I love."

He grunts, "I swear. You're the most challenging woman I've ever met."

I smile, "Jameson, you'd never be happy with a boring woman. That's why no one caught you before now."

He grabs my ass in his palm. "God help me. I have a feeling I'm in for a long, hard road."

I reach back and wrap his thick cock in my palm. "Amen to long and hard."

We barely make it to the bed. But it's perfect. I wouldn't want it any other way. And when I fall asleep, I'm in bliss knowing he's beside me. Protecting me. Loving me.

Yep. I just thought the L word.

## CHAPTER FORTY-THREE

*Scotch*

Morning comes too fast. I don't want to let her get dressed. Or let her go. But time's up. When we walk into the other hotel room, Mako's tapping on his laptop at the small desk, his face in a hard scowl. "Alright. I just need a few of photos of you, Wolf."

He pulls out a cell phone as Wolf walks over. Mako stands and takes a frontal face shot, then zooms in on his cheek, catching an image of the birthmark. "Now, hold this paper up so I can capture the headline."

Wolf rolls his eyes and mutters. "We still have to do this? I know we do, but I mean, you'd think in this decade we'd have some other way of providing a date stamp. I know digital date stamps can be altered, but sheesh. Bloody last century bullshit. What happens when papers go away for good?"

## CHAPTER 43

Mako grumbles as he angles for another photo. "Tell me about it, I had to walk five blocks to find a newspaper stand."

When the photos are done, both men go back to work on their laptops.

"So, what's the timeline?" Simona asks.

"I'm pushing to make this happen fast. I'm going to upload the photos now, send them to the buyer, and get things rolling."

Two hours later, Simona and I are in our nearby hotel room when we get the call.

I put the phone on speaker. It's Mako. "It's set. We're meeting for the exchange in six hours. Marshall and the others will be back just in time."

"Where's this happening?"

"Right here in England."

In the background, Wolf yells, "My stomping grounds, mate!"

Simona leans over the phone. "Perfect. At least someone knows the lay of the land."

"So, what now?"

Mako says, "We take a little drive. Get set up near the exchange site."

Simona hops up. "Roger that. We'll be ready in five."

As the nerves in my gut hit high alert, I confirm and disconnect. The needle on the clock is ticking. I'm just thankful as hell that it will be Mako and Wolf walking into that exchange.

\* \* \*

There's two hours left when we stop at a small Inn somewhere deep in the countryside.

Mako rolls down his window. "Let's grab a couple of rooms and lay low."

"Roger that."

Simona and I walk in and book a room. Mako follows immediately after. We gather in our room for some last-minute plans.

Wolf pulls up a satellite image on his computer. "So, this is how it's going down. The exchange is supposed to take place at this gate." He points to a mark on the screen. "This building here, this is a guard shack. This one is a mansion, but it's actually just an empty shell. The real facility is behind this, a half mile down a country lane."

"Wow, elaborate place. How do you know this?"

"I have a good connection. This place has been on the radar for a while as being suspicious."

Simona asks, "What goes on there?"

"Nothing like smuggling or commerce, but this man, he's got some kind of multibillion dollar business."

I whistle, "Wow, and he's taking a chance on bringing this right to his front door."

Wolf nods and grins. "Not very smart, huh?"

Simona groans, "I hope I didn't inherit that fatal flaw."

I stretch out the tension in my neck. "Where are the rest of the team?"

Mako checks his watch. "ETA, one hour."

"Too damned close for my taste."

Simona bumps my shoulder with hers. "They're always on time." I just hope they are this time.

Wolf closes his laptop, "I've got this. Don't worry. This is my kind of gig."

"You're just going to grab this man, whoever he is, in the midst of his place, in the middle of his secured estate."

## CHAPTER 43

"Yep. And I'm going to do it before the trade goes down."

Simona gasps. "How in the world?"

"They don't call me Shadow for nothing."

Her eyes brighten. "You're going to have to teach me about these tricks you use."

Wolf grins. "You're keen on it, huh?"

I clear my throat and give Wolf my most threatening glare. Wolf's face falls serious. "Maybe I won't. I'm not having your surgeon there sizing me up for a lobotomy. Or a whatever 'ectomy.' I like keeping all my parts in place."

Simona huffs and flashes murderous eyes at me. "Fine. I'm fine without your help."

Wolf starts packing his gear, checking his vest, gun, and other tactical tools while Simona watches. I try to keep my eyes off the clock. But I suck at it because every second feels like we are getting closer to some cataclysm.

Wolf slings his backpack on his shoulder. "Alright. I think I'm ready, Mako. Let's do this."

Mako pulls his coat over his holster. "You two stay here on standby in case Wolf needs a pick up from some other location."

Simona's wringing her hands and pacing back and forth. "I can't believe I have to stay here!"

Wolf reaches out to shake my hand. "See you in a bit, mate. Keep an eye on this one."

Then he hugs her. "Take it easy, don't wear a hole through to the floor below, Sprite."

"Not funny. Be safe. I just met you. I have lots of things to pry from your brain, so hurry back."

Mako opens the door and the two men step out into the hallway. When the door closes, I find Simona staring at me. She's fuming. "This sucks."

"This is safe."

She flops onto the bed on her back. Grumbling something in Czech.

I pull back the curtain and watch Mako and Wolf cross the parking lot. As they reach the car, Wolf holds up his hand as he takes a call. He paces across the narrow pavement. Nodding. Saying something into the phone.

He must feel my eyes on him because he looks right up at me. He makes a slicing motion across his neck, then starts running toward the Inn.

Fuck. Something bad is happening.

# CHAPTER FORTY-FOUR

*Scotch*

Wolf and Mako storm back into the room.

With a hand in his short-cropped hair, Wolf says, "We have a problem. *Fucking motherfucker*. I knew this could happen. I have to go on deployment. I have to leave NOW. This mission is ultra time sensitive. I was hoping we could get this done before anything came up. But when command says I have to go, there's no way out of it."

Simona covers her eyes with her palms. "Oh. No! That's *not* good."

Mako slides his laptop across the desk and throws himself into the chair. "There's not much time to figure out what we're going to do."

When Simona jumps up and exclaims, "I'll go." My head nearly explodes.

"Fuck no!"

She grabs Mako's arm. "I'll go. I can get in there and you guys and the rest of the Agile Team can take this guy out."

Wolf looks at me with utter disbelief on his face. "Is she always this crazy?"

I clench my jaw so hard my neck cracks. "You're only seeing half of the crazy right now."

Simona waves a hand dismissively. "Just show up with me. Send photos of me too. Tell him you can only bring one at a time. It's too much to manage us both. He can give you the money for the easy one first. Being that I'm a woman and all that you'll be able to deal with me easier."

Mako shakes his head. "He'll never buy it. I've already said I have the male. I've sent the photos."

Simona and Mako start shouting at each other.

I slam my hand down on the desk. "I'm going in with Mako. Not you, Simona. End of discussion. I'll stand in for Wolf. We're close enough in size."

A tsunami of silence crashes over the room. Simona and Mako just stare at me.

Her in horror. Him in satisfaction.

Wolf clasps my shoulder with a hard grip. "I'm sorry as fuck about this. But I have to move out. If anything changes before the time you meet that fucker, I'll be back."

I shake his hand. "I've got it. Just keep your hide safe so she doesn't haunt you in your grave."

# CHAPTER FORTY-FIVE

## Simona

"Don't. No. Don't go. We'll figure something else out." I can barely breathe. My lungs are locked up tight as a new kind of fear takes hold of me.

"I'm going. We can have this done with once and for all." The hard light in Scotch's eyes tells me this is already off of the table. It's done. And I have no control over this careening freight train.

Mako and Scotch go over every minute detail as I pace and fume and fidget. By the time they are done, I'm literally shaking so hard I could vibrate the building. What if Scotch can't remember all the fake background info that Mako cooked up about the man he's bringing in.

As he starts to put on his jacket, I grab the thick wool lapels. "Are you sure you remember all of the details?"

His eyes soften as he rests a hand on my cheek. The man's infuriatingly calm. "Yes, babe. Ask me something."

"What is your birth sign?"

"Gemini."

"What college did you go to?"

Mako interrupts. "Time to roll everyone. Simona, you know where to park and wait."

"Yes," I say with my teeth practically chattering.

With a soft kiss, Scotch says, "Babe. Your idea to lure them out of the compound was perfect. This is going to go seamlessly. We'll fake our car breaking down on the way, and they have to come meet us in an open space. Then we'll have the advantage."

My voice is reedy and my knees are weak when I say, "I hope so." I suck at this. Send me in any day. Watching someone I care about going into a potential nightmare turns me into a raving lunatic.

Scotch hugs me hard. "You've got my back. I'm in great hands."

"I remember you telling me once not to shoot you."

He grins wickedly. "I remember that. Same applies this time. Now go. I'll see you soon. I love you, little vixen."

The L word rattles my brain for half a second. He grins. Smacks me with another kiss to the cheek.

I hug him once more before I run out the door because if I stay, I'll chain him to me, just like he threatened to do to me. "I love you too. Now hurry back. We've got a baby to raise together."

He watches me back away with his expression filled with something so big, that I have to look away.

As I fly down the stairs, my throat is so tight with tears I almost can't breathe.

I dial my phone the instant I hit the outdoors. "Marshall. Where the hell are you?"

"Weather delay."

# CHAPTER 45

"Please tell me you're going to be here on time."

"Doing our best. Slow things down if you can."

"We're working on that. I've got to go. I'm driving like I'm in a rally race right now. I wish Andre was here."

"Good god, Sprite. Hang up."

I can't. I'm concentrating on the road, so he disconnects. Mashing the little accelerator and grinding the gears, I drive like a possessed woman, pushing the little rental car to its limits through the winding English countryside.

When I make my stakeout spot, there's only one vehicle parked in the overlook. A couple of kids are making out in the front seat of an old truck.

Discreetly, I pull the binoculars out and wait for signs of Mako and Scotch on the road below as my heart tries viciously to destroy my sternum.

I can't imagine what kind of go-juice the baby is getting right now. Super-stress hormones can't be good for the little thing.

Taking a few breaths, I try to get my center back. But holy hell— When the man you can't do without is down there being exchanged for two million dollars, how is a girl supposed to keep her shit together?

Breathe.

Breathe.

Breathe.

The blue rented sedan they are driving finally appears in the distance. It winds slowly through the twists and turns in the dull gray winter landscape.

Pretending the car is losing power, Mako slows and speeds the thing at irregular intervals. Finally, it comes to a stop in front of me. A hillside several hundred yards long and small stream separate us. Mako climbs out. He pops the hood and sticks his head under, pretending to fidget with something. I know Scotch is 'tied up' in the back seat, but I can't see him.

I frantically dial Marshall's satellite phone again. "Where are you?"

"Waiting for clearance to land the jet."

I can't even reply, I'm so upset.

"Sprite. We're coming as quickly as we can. What's happening on the ground?"

"Mako and Scotch are in place. It looks like Mako is on the phone right now. Calling the target."

"Copy. I'll update you as soon as we land." The line goes dead and I drop my head to the steering wheel. Tears well in my eyes.

This is so jacked, I can't sit here and let them do this without cover. I'm too far away here. If I had a sniper rifle... And sniper training. I could do something.

I slip on my coat and stuff an extra ammo clip in the back of my jeans. When Mako's looking the other way, I slide from the car. Hugging the tree line, I start a slow descent.

# CHAPTER FORTY-SIX

*Scotch*

Mako's voice carries to me through the car windows. Sounds like our plan is working.

After a few minutes of doing something under the hood, he climbs back in the car and tries to start it. The cable he unhooked keeps it from firing over.

"They bought it."

We worked out the details before, but now that it's almost time, it feels wise to revisit.

"Good. We'll see how it goes. If Daddy dearest really cares about his kids, then he's going to be easy to get close to. Then I can subdue him while you take care of any goons he might have along for the ride."

Mako sits forward suddenly. "Looks like it's game time. We got a limo at ten o'clock. Moving fast."

"Just one?"

"Yep."

I blow out a breath. "Good, this is very good."

"Alright, they're stopping just up ahead. Here we go."

Mako levers himself out of the small car. Holding onto the open door, he throws up a hand. "Hello!"

Under his breath, he mutters, "A driver, a guard, and a man in a suit are walking this way."

"Good day," Mako says in a cheery voice.

I can't hear the other person's reply.

"Sure. He's in the back. What would you like for me to do?"

Mako shifts and closes his door, he opens the rear passenger door where I'm seated. "Out you go."

He grabs my arm and pulls me out. Careful to keep the cheek that should have the mark turned slightly, I climb to my feet.

Mako pushes me in front of him. "Here's your man."

Standing just ahead of us are two men. One obviously security. Big as a house, his pistol is already in his hand.

The other is remarkably like Wolf. Grayer, but just as fit. Just as agile-looking. I never thought about having to wrestle a man of Wolf's physical stature to the ground. That may have been a serious miscalculation.

The smile the man flashes at me is chilling. Feral. The idea of this man getting close to Simona makes my skin shrink. "Son. Come to me. Let me get a closer look at you."

With my hands fake tied behind my back, I say, "Excuse me? I don't know what you're talking about."

The man straightens his jacket. "You're my son. I said, come to me."

I take a step toward him. "How can I be your son? I have parents. And you're not one of them."

"It's a long story. One we can discuss over cocktails. It's

## CHAPTER 46

time for you to come home. Untie him." He motions toward the guard. "And give the man his money."

The guard moves to untie me, but Mako stops him. "Here, I'll do it. I used a special knot. Just get my money while I do it."

The guard grunts and turns back to the car. Stupid move.

This is our chance.

The second the rope drops from my hands, I leap for the man who claims he's my father. My attack surprises him and I get the upper hand. Locking him in a chokehold, I wrestle him to the ground. With a perfectly placed lock, I knock him unconscious. *God,* I love that trick.

Mako's standing off with the guard when I look up. Oh hell.

"Drop your weapon." The big bodyguard shouts.

Mako laughs. "You first."

The door to the limo swings open, and a skinny driver half falls out of the car. With shaking legs, he holds up a pistol. From the way he's holding the thing, I'm ninety-nine percent certain he's never shot a gun.

Great, just what we need. Barney Fife on the scene.

The ground suddenly starts to rumble, and the air turns viscous, suddenly, as wind whips around us. The deafening roar of a helicopter swoops in on us.

Dirt flies off the ground, in my eyes, in my mouth. Holding my hand up, I try to make out what's happening.

From above, an English voice rumbles through a speaker. "Drop your weapon now or be fired on."

I stare in disbelief as one SAS soldier after another fast-ropes down to the ground. In seconds, we're surrounded, and the bodyguard is face down on the ground. The driver is on his knees with his hands in the air and a look on his face that says he'll never leave the house again.

I turn to search for Simona on the hillside above, in the place where she's supposed to be waiting. But I can't see her. The car is there, but she's not visible.

Suddenly, I'm hit broadside by a hug so fierce it knocks me sideways.

She's hysterical. "*Ohmygod ohmygod.*"

I grab the woman who stole my heart and pull her into my arms. "It's okay, babe. Everything is just fine." She buries her face in my chest.

"Never. Ever. *Ever*. Do that again."

"I don't plan on it. Now, come on. We've got someone to thank."

Clasping her hand, I pull her into the midst of the chaos. We find Wolf, decked in tan camo and tactical gear, standing next to the handcuffed bodyguard. He's talking to one of the other troops.

When the other man leaves, I offer a grin. "I didn't expect to see you here."

He laughs as he glances up at the hovering helicopter. "Change of plans. We were in the neighborhood, so I thought we'd drop by."

"Good timing, man. Thanks."

"You're welcome. Now we'll get some answers out of that son of a bitch, if you didn't kill him, that is."

We turn toward the other man, the 'father.' He's on the ground. One of the SAS guys is prodding him with his boot. "He's just unconscious."

Simona pulls out of my hold. "At last! Now I get in on the action."

## CHAPTER FORTY-SEVEN

## Simona

Right as the SAS team helps us break into the giant compound of Willem Swartz, the Agile team arrives. Together in a coordinated effort, we all sweep the grounds.

I feel like I'm in some weird movie as we find five other siblings. All locked in well-appointed bedrooms, hostage to the madman.

Each one of them is unique, but so much like Wolf and me.

Three men. Two women. All between twenty-seven and twenty-nine. All of them are confused, angry, and ready to go back to their normal lives after months of being held against their will.

Now we are seven.

Seven souls brought together by a madman. Seven individuals with rattled memories and futures that are now intertwined in the most unexpected way.

A small bus arrives and I see that they all get loaded on for the trip to the Inn where Marshall secured lodging and a place for debriefing. But I stay behind to be with the team until everything is finished.

I get a small amount of closure when I watch the man who is my biological father taken away by authorities in cuffs and shackles. It's obvious he's very mentally ill. Since he came around, he's been spouting his insanity to anyone that would listen. The officer in charge assures me he's going to get help.

Scotch finds me on the steps by the circular drive. Watching as the police cars drive away. He pulls me against his side in a warm hug that I so need. "Sweetheart, I know this is a lot to absorb."

"My god. I'm numb, honestly."

"That man is a sick bastard."

"Can you believe he paid that doctor to inseminate all of those poor unknowing women with fertilized eggs he had designed to produce his ideal offspring? My heart just breaks for my mother. She had no idea what was happening to her when she just turned up pregnant."

"It's an atrocity. Do you know how he got the eggs?"

"Not yet. With some luck, we'll be able to track down the source. I can't imagine what that woman would think to find this out. Eight of us survived to birth, but there would have been more if all the pregnancies had taken hold."

"And he just thought you all would willingly become members of his grand scheme?"

"Yes. His fantasy was to take over the world's supply of some rare earth minerals used in technology. Having his family surrounding him as both mental and physical soldiers was his sick way to make that happen. He had this elaborate plan on how all of us would bring our skills to his inner circle. But I think my siblings had other thoughts."

"Sounds like he was disappointed in them?"

I smile at the thought of them popping his bubble. "Yep, when they called him a lunatic and refused to help, he got quite angry."

Wolf strides over, his assault rifle slung across his chest. He's an intimidating looking man, but I can tell he's a lot more relaxed. Just like I feel.

He turns to watch one of the police cars leave. "Well, I guess all are accounted for, except one sister. Swartz says that the last one, a woman, hasn't been located. I'm guessing somehow her birth records were lost like mine were, or her name changed like yours did."

Excited at the idea of the search, I say. "I'm going to track her down as quickly as I can."

My brother says, "I think that's a good plan, it will give you something to do while you nurture that little bambino that you and my brother-in-law made."

I laugh at him, but my insides turn to a nervous knot. "Whoa there. We're barely even dating. There have been no talks of marriage."

Good god. Marriage.

I can barely say the L word without getting tongue-tied. How am I supposed to think about marriage?

Wolf tips his chin toward Scotch. "I can't imagine those talks will be too far off."

Scotch kisses the top of my head. "Your brother's a smart man, babe. Now, let's get the hell out of here and get on with the rest of our life."

# CHAPTER FORTY-EIGHT

## Simona

The Inn's tiny restaurant is full of people. The majority of them look like me or Wolf. It's kind of dizzying, actually.

"We need name tags," Sierra says as she breezes by.

"No joke. I can't keep everyone's name straight."

After the debriefing, it's been non-stop talk.

This brother is talking to that one.

Sisters huddled together.

Little groups morph and morph, over and over again, until it's all a blur of laughter, tears, and hugs. The racket in the small pub is beautiful and fills my heart to the brim.

I can't believe I just acquired six—maybe seven—siblings in less than twenty-four hours.

Talk about mind-blowing. A girl who never had much of a family—well, except for Josef—now has a whole pub full of relatives. I can't wait to introduce the man who raised me to all of them.

## CHAPTER 48

But as much as I want to spend hour upon hour talking to every single one of them, I want to be alone with my man—the brave doctor who put his life on the line to bring closure to the threat that was hanging over my head.

Again, he saved me.

I'm overwhelmed by him.

The ferocity of his bravery. His desire for me.

When I told my two new sisters that I just found out I was pregnant, they cried beautiful tears of joy. It nearly made my heart explode.

It felt so right to share this with them, even though trusting has never been easy for me.

After, I excused myself to splash my face after our love fest. When I walk back in, Scotch catches my eye from across the bar. Without dropping his focus, he makes his way to me. "Hey, beautiful."

"Hey there, handsome doctor."

"What are you thinking about?"

"That our baby is going to have a lot of aunts and uncles."

He grins as he leans down to brush his lips across mine. "And probably a lot of cousins someday. And lots of baby sitters."

I smile against his lips. "I like the way you think."

His hand skims along my waist and drops lower where he suggestively squeezes my hip bone. "What do you say we blow this joint?"

"I say, lead the way."

When he folds my arm in his and leads me out, he's smiling in that way that makes my heart squeeze.

I'm pretty sure we look like two lovestruck fools as we race up the steps.

He drops the key by accident. I bend to grab it, but I'm

laughing so hard I can't see the slot to put it in. He growls and picks me up. "Give me that damned key before I have to kick this door in. I can't wait another minute to be inside of you."

I finally, finally get the key to work. He bursts in the door and tosses me on the bed. I bounce dangerously close to the edge, but he catches me, pinning me below his big body.

Our hands tangle as we rip at each other's clothes. He's growling like a feral animal. I'm giggling until he takes my mouth by storm. Then I'm whisked into a world of raging desire and emotion so strong it makes it hard to breathe.

Thrusting against my tongue, he claims me. The kiss is glorious, long, and heart-stopping. "Mine," he growls when he pulls away.

Then he throws my right leg over his arm and shoves his giant cock into me. "Fuck, Simona, you make me a possessive, hungry, crazy mother fucker."

With a powerful contraction of his big body, he drives into me again. Hanging on, I dig my fingers into his thick shoulders. Quickly, he has me moaning as my eyes roll back. "God. Scotch. *Yes*."

It feels sooo good. I can't even find my words. He strokes into me from tip to base, over and over, stretching me, loving me, driving us closer to the brink of something bigger than ever before.

Shifting me, he folds me tighter in his embrace. I love it. Love it so much. The warmth. The strength. Pressing his forehead against mine, he whispers words of love. Praise. Possession.

I've never experienced anything so sexy and intimate in my life.

This man. He undoes me.

## CHAPTER 48

Nothing will ever do, but him loving me.

When I'm on the brink of shattering, he catches my face between his hands. His voice is low and thick with his desire. "Look at me as we come together."

His dark brown eyes are on fire. They lock me to him. Forever.

I lick across my trembling lips. I can't speak.

He shifts his thrusts until he's just on that perfect spot and I begin to shudder.

"That's it. Let go. Surrender your pleasure to me."

Sounds I've never made come from my throat.

"God, you're so damned beautiful," he growls as he moves that incredible body against me in perfect rhythm. A fluid glide of muscles in the golden lamplight.

I try to nod, tell him I'm almost there, but I can't move as all burning pleasure rolls through me in a heavy wave. Tears leak from my eyes and run down my cheeks.

"Ah!" His pace quickens. His voice is a rough, throaty growl. "*Now*. Come with me."

Oh! Yes. I come. And come. And when he murmurs three unexpected words, "We are one," I come undone all over again.

\* \* \*

THE PHONE RINGS on the bedside table. I peel my eyes open. The room's empty. *Hm.*

My voice barely works when I try to answer. "Hello."

"Time for breakfast, sexy. Come down to the pub. Everyone's here."

My eyes are full of sleep. Every muscle is deliciously sore as I stretch beneath the sheet and heavy blanket. "What time is it?"

"Eight. Come on down."

"Alright. I'll be there as soon as I find my brain. You seem to have screwed it right out of me."

He laughs. The sound is warm and toe curling. "Glad I could be of service. See you in a few." He clicks the line off.

Damn. So much for snuggling in bed all morning.

But... breakfast does sound damn good. I'm starving.

I take a record-fast two-minute shower, toss my wet hair into a ponytail and put on the same clothes I had yesterday since I don't have anything else.

I hit the steps at a run. When I land on the lobby level, I can see that everyone is already inside the pub.

Wow. Bunch of early risers.

I pop in the door.

And freeze. Everyone's staring at me... with weird looks on their faces.

Scotch steps around Wolf and holds out a hand. "Come on in."

My nerves fizzle in my belly. "*Uh*. What's up?"

I'm sure my eyes nearly leave my face when Scotch drops to his knee on the scuffed wooden pub floor. He pulls my hand into his and kisses it gently.

"Oh. *My*. God." I must be asleep. This is some kind of weird dream.

But it feels really real. Scotch's face is shockingly serious as he looks up at me. *Oh lord*. This *really* is happening.

He opens his hand and in the center of his palm is a sparkling diamond ring. It's incredible. Smooth and sleek with the fiery diamond embedded right into the band. I'm officially stunned.

"Simona Novotny, will you be my wife?"

The room is so quiet I'm sure everyone can hear my

## CHAPTER 48

heart spasming inside of my chest. I will not faint. I will *not* faint.

My voice comes out as a squeak, "Me?"

He nods, "You. The one and only. My heart won't stand for any other."

"Oh, Scotch." I touch his strong, handsome face with my fingertips. "*Yes!* Yes. I'll be Mrs. Jameson Scott."

The room explodes in cheers. We're swarmed by yelling and clapping. If anyone else in the building was sleeping, they'll be running for the fire escapes.

Before I can catch my breath, Scotch spins me in a circle as he presses his face into my neck. He's laughing man tears against me and I swear he sounds like the happiest man in the world when he says, "Welcome to the crazy train."

## CHAPTER FORTY-NINE

*Scotch*

### Three Months Later

She has no idea where we're going. This makes me feel highly accomplished. It's hard to pull much off on her.

I turn onto route 417, then left onto a little gravel road.

"Okay, you've officially got me curious."

"Just be patient."

"I have been for an hour. You've driven all over."

"Have I?"

At the end of the road, a small patch of grass has been cut in the middle of a field. "What's that?'

"Oh, nothing."

I turn the truck off.

"What are we doing?"

"Waiting."

## CHAPTER 49

She groans and throws her head back against the headrest. "You're a handful."

I chuckle at this. She often tells me how I'm more than a handful, and more than a mouthful.

I roll down the window. "Hear that?"

Her eyes brighten up. "What is that?"

"You'll see."

She watches me with something between curiosity and frustration.

The grass in front of us begins to swirl as the sound of the chopper fills the cab of the truck.

"What in the world?"

"Our ride."

"Where are we going?"

"You'll see."

I hop from the truck and she meets me out front as Larson lowers his private bird to the ground.

We run hand in hand to the chopper. Lifting Simona up, I place her into the back seating area. I climb in beside her. As soon as we are settled, we put on our headsets.

"Hello, lovebirds," Larson says with a grin.

Simona's smiling really big. "I'm really confused now."

"Just sit back and relax. Everything is taken care of."

As we fly across the mountains, I can't pull my eyes off her. The excitement in her face nearly explodes my heart.

It takes thirty minutes by air to reach the cabin I've rented for the wedding. Larson takes us to our destination and begins circling as we planned. "Remember when you told me to put together a wedding because the idea of it was too stressful for you?"

Her lashes fly apart. "You didn't!"

"I didn't do it by myself. But it's done."

She glances down. "Oh my god, Scotch, right now? You

told me to wear a dress, but I didn't know you meant a wedding dress."

I lean over and kiss the adorable expression on her sweet, perfect mouth. "Taken care of. I got the one you picked out in the little shop in town. Nolene Strong and Sierra made sure it was all taken care of."

Her eyes well up with tears. "*Oh,* Scotch."

I wrap her hand up in mine. "Now, that's all I'm telling you."

She wipes at her tears with her free hand. "My god, you know how to surprise a girl."

"Those are my goals, to always keep you guessing and smiling."

The grounds of the property are buzzing with activity. Everyone's already arrived. The aisle is marked with fresh flowers and ferns. White and navy ribbons dance in the air around the gazebo as the chopper lowers to the ground nearby.

We're met at the edge of the lawn by a herd of friends and family. Simona's crying happy tears as her two sisters hug her. "Oh my! Look at all these beautiful people."

"This is so exciting!" the taller of the three, Mariana, says, as she rushes Simona off to the house to get changed.

I couldn't look away if I had to. And she must feel me. Simona turns to wave at me from the porch as she smoothes her hand down over her little baby bump. She blows me a kiss.

Andre punches me in the arm. "You are a lucky fucker."

"Tell me about it. Thanks for coming."

"Wouldn't have missed it."

"Did you meet the sisters?"

He chuckles. "I might have said hello."

"Good."

# CHAPTER 49

Josef crosses the lawn toward us as Wolf walks up. The older man is smiling as he tips his head. "Gentlemen."

"Simona hasn't seen you yet."

The older man grins. "I'm quite looking forward to surprising her when she comes out to walk down the aisle."

Wolf chuckles. "Poor girl. She's just getting it from every angle."

Josef waves a dismissive hand. "If you know how long I've been trying to surprise that girl, you'd understand. She's wiser than any owl."

We share a laugh.

Then Josef says, "Boys, would you mind if I have a moment alone with Jameson?"

They bow out and I'm left with Simona's closest friend and father figure. "Thank you for giving me permission to ask for her hand."

"Of course. I knew the first time I saw you that you were worthy of her."

That thickens my throat. "Thanks. That means a lot."

"Look, I hope you'll consider spending some time in Czech. I'd like to get to be a part of things with you, her, and my grandchild."

"Already planning that."

He nods. "Good." From the inside of his jacket, he produces an envelope.

"What's this?"

"Just a little something for the newlyweds."

"Thank you. I'll wait to open it with Simona."

He pats my shoulder. "Look out for my girl. I've got sources, you know, that will tell me if you're not keeping up your end of the deal." He chuckles as he walks off.

I shake my head. "Guess I should have expected as much," I mutter as I walk off toward the gazebo.

There I find my father talking with Marshall. I'm sure my surprise shows. "Hey, you decided to come."

He frowns, "Of course I did."

"It means a lot."

Marshall passes me the garment bag that holds my suit, then leaves me alone with the man I haven't seen in who knows how many years.

"This is quite the place. That view." He nods his now gray head toward the horizon. "Postcard material."

I know he's just making small talk because we're both about as brittle as old plastic right now.

"It's pretty incredible. Just like Simona."

"She's a beautiful girl."

Silence falls between us.

He kicks at the grass below his shoe. "You seem happy."

"I am. I'm in love. It feels damn good."

"And your career?"

Ah, I knew it was coming. "What about it?"

"Are you done practicing medicine?"

"No, never will be, I suspect."

He shifts, pushes his hands into his pant pockets. "I heard you saved her life in San Miguel."

I nod. "Yep. Was stressful as hell."

"You're a damned fine surgeon. I've been told by many."

I'm not sure how to reply to that.

He clears his throat. "Look. I know that there's history between us about this. When I told you that you couldn't do it, I was at a very bad place in my life. In my heart, I knew you could, I always knew you'd be a better doctor than me, I just didn't know if I could give you what you needed to get you there. Raising you alone was hard. I fucked up a lot. And somehow, against all odds, here you are. You survived it all. And came out on top. I'm damned proud of that."

Well, fuck. I clear my throat. Twice. "I'm shocked to hear you say that."

"I understand. And nothing will make up for the pain I caused back then. But if you'll have my offer, I'd like to get to know the man you've become."

He steps in and hugs me then. For a solid minute, I can't move as pain tries to shake itself loose from my heart. Finally, I manage to say, "I'd like that."

"You better go get ready. Your bride is going to be looking for you."

I blink back the moisture in my eyes. "You're right. Let's talk after. I wanted to introduce you to Simona."

He smiles wistfully. "I'd like that."

The next twenty minutes pass in a blur. Marshall knocks on the bedroom door where I dressed. "It's time, brother."

When I open the door, he looks a little rattled. "What's wrong?"

"Weddings give me the willies."

I laugh. "They used to do that to me too."

"Well, I'm pretty sure your fiancée isn't going to leave you on the altar."

I know my face falls flat. "You do know I'm marrying Simona. This wouldn't be the first time she took off."

He rolls his eyes. "She's still getting ready, I checked."

I let out a breath. "Whew, okay."

"Come on. Get your ass down to the gazebo."

"Man, you couldn't keep me away if you tried."

He follows me as I head down the stairs toward the most important meeting of my life.

## CHAPTER FIFTY

## Simona

Nolene Strong taps her foot as she curls the last strand of my hair. When she lets the blonde ringlet slide off the iron, she steps back to study her handwork. "Now, that's lovely."

She passes me a hand mirror. I'm so delighted all I can do is nod and watch the beautiful curls slide against my shoulders.

My sisters, Mariana and Gilly, help me into my dress. I feel like a fairy princess. A very pampered one.

"Scotch did an outstanding job," Nolene remarks as she picks up my bouquet, a big bunch of lavender roses wrapped in deep navy silk ribbon.

"I know. I'm so thrilled." I lift my arms out to the side as Mariana zips up my strapless floor-length gown. Its simple cut and elegant silk fabric are what made me fall in love with it instantly. "One of the things that terrified me about a wedding was all of the details. Before Sierra and Cole's wedding I'd never even been to one. How was I supposed to plan one?"

Gilly gasps. "You're lying?"

"Nope. I didn't exactly have a lot of girlfriends. And no sisters... well, until now."

My oldest sister's face goes sad suddenly, for a second, before she smiles again. "Have you found her yet?"

"No. But I got some good intel. I have a feeling it won't be long now."

Mariana lowers a crown of delicate white flowers to my head. "We'll just have to have a great big party when you do find her. Maybe when the baby is born."

"I love that idea!"

Nolene pushes a few bobby pins in to hold my headpiece in place. Then she passes me my bouquet. "That baby bump makes you look even more adorable."

I grin. "It is pretty cute, isn't it?"

The girls chatter away about my growing tummy while I apply some lip stuff. Gilly puts on my mascara, the only other thing I'm wearing beside Scotch's favorite lip gloss. The strawberry one.

I smack my lips. "Alright, girls, I think that's a wrap. And to think I didn't have to worry about a single thing. I still can't believe he pulled this off."

Nolene laughs as she swings the door open. "That boy's a keeper."

"That's my plan."

At the bottom of the stairs, I take a moment to look in the full-length mirror.

Wow. *This* is me.

Who would have thought the scrawny teenager living in the streets, digging in the trash, would be a fairy princess with her very own Prince Charming?

I turn my head when I catch movement out of the corner of my eye. My heart leaps into my throat. "Josef!"

He laughs and kisses my hand. "My child. You are the most lovely bride in the world."

"I can't believe you're here."

"Your fiancé is a man of many talents."

I know I'm grinning like a fool. "He is."

"Come along, my dear. I'm escorting you down the aisle to your future husband."

"Really? Why would you do that?"

"It's customary, my dear."

He offers his arm again.

"Oh. I didn't know that someone would escort me."

Josef's brow quirks up on an angle. "I see that I failed in some parts of your education."

I slide my hand into the bend of his arm. "Not on the important parts."

When we step from the house, the party on the lawn grows quiet. The musicians begin playing a song that's so lovely my eyes tear up. Josef pats my hand. We walk together down the stairs and down the brick pathway to the gazebo.

Everything is so beautiful, but nothing matters except the amazing man waiting at the end of the aisle. He's my everything.

So handsome in his suit, he steals my breath. My god. This man is mine. Forever.

I'm so floaty, high on happiness, I barely even register when Josef passes my hand to Scotch. The next thing I know, we are alone at the base of the gazebo. My fiancé leans down, touches his sexy lips to mine. "Mine. All mine," he whispers as he pulls away. "Come this way, my dear."

## CHAPTER 50

Together, we step into the gazebo where a man is waiting. He smiles as we approach.

Savannah, Sierra, Mariana, and Gilly join us on one side. Liam, Andre, Marshall, and Wolf stand with Scotch.

I can't hold back the smile that makes my cheeks ache.

The minister tells me what to say, I try to follow as my heart hums along at a happy clip near the speed of sound. We share our promises of love and togetherness.

Scotch gently glides a beautiful gold band onto my finger next to the diamond ring he gave me in England. With trembling fingers, I slide a thick dark metal band on his.

The whole time, he never takes his serious focus off me. As if I'm the only thing in the world.

Scotch is so steady. And strong and present. Like he always is.

"You may now kiss the bride!"

I blink. "Oh! That's it?"

Everyone in the gazebo laughs. Scotch's devastating smile makes my knees weak, but he's got me in his arms, so I have not a fear in the world. "You're officially married to me now."

I vaguely hear cheers as he bends me back over his arm and kisses me until I'm breathless. Another of his many skills. Reducing me to putty in his arms.

He tips me back up and wraps his arm around my waist. "Our friends and family are waiting for us, Mrs. Jameson Scott."

"Oh, I do like the way that sounds."

And just like that, the next chapter of my life opens. And I just know in my heart it's going to be as glorious as any fairytale.

## CHAPTER FIFTY-ONE

*Scotch*

"I've never broken a plate on purpose."

Simona laughs. "My sisters said this is a Czech tradition that we have to keep."

"Alright. Here we go." I slam a perfectly good plate on the ground. It feels surprisingly good to watch it shatter.

Together, we clean it up, me sweeping, her holding the broom. Apparently this is all part of the old tradition. The crowd cheers and jokes as we make a show of it.

"Teamwork," she says with a delighted laugh.

"I think we've got that part down pretty good, my dear."

When the show is over, I take her hand. "Let's take a stroll."

She joins me, wrapping her arm in mine. I love the feel of her hand tucked along the inside of my arm.

## CHAPTER 51

"I want to show you something."

We walk to the edge of the hillside to look out over the amazing vista. The valley plunges far below like a blanket of green and gold. I take her to the bench that's placed for enjoying this breathtaking view.

"One of the reasons I picked this place for the wedding is because of the view."

"It's unreal. Breathtaking, really."

"And special," I say as I pass her the pair of binoculars I had stashed here for the wedding.

"Take a look down there." I point. "Just at the edge of the ridge, before you drop down into the valley floor. There's a red barn there. Move about four hundred yards to the left of that."

"It looks like... construction?"

"Look closely."

"A house is being framed."

"Not just any house."

She lowers the binoculars and worries at her lip. "What kind of house is it?"

"Ours."

Those big blue eyes of hers flare. "Our house." She buries her face back in the binoculars. "That's our house?"

"Yes, it will be done in a few months. Larson's building it."

"I've never had a house."

I chuckle. "Me either."

She's all breathy and excited. "It's going to be amazing. I can tell already."

"It's not gigantic. But it's special."

She sets the binos aside and catches my face between her hands. "Yes, it is. And. I. Love. You."

"I know you might feel a little claustrophobic. So, I made some plans to help with that."

She brushes her thumb over my cheek. "I used to think that, but now, I know I'm happy as long as I'm with you."

I pass her a piece of paper from my pocket.

She studies the text on it. "Plane tickets."

"A month-long honeymoon in Europe. We'll pick out an apartment there as well. Something that can serve as our second home base."

Her eyes mist up. "You thought of everything."

"I tried."

She kisses me. Slowly, as her arms wrap around my neck. "I love you, Jameson. Husband. Lover. Lifesaver."

When she pulls back, I dig into my pocket. "I almost forgot. Josef gave me this. He said it's a present for us."

She takes the envelope. When she opens it, she laughs. "That man."

"Are you going to tell me?"

"He... he gave us a deed to the cabin where you found me." She reads the note that's enclosed, translating for me. "I'm so very happy for you both. And I give you this, a place for you to be close so we can make some new family memories. I'm very excited to be a grandfather. Of course, this is a wonderful place to base your European operations too."

She squeezes the letter against her heart. "I'm overwhelmed."

"He loves you."

"And he loves you too, apparently."

"I'm glad. I don't want to end up in the holding cell in the basement."

Her eyes shine as she wraps her fingers tighter in mine. "I know where he keeps the key."

## CHAPTER 51

With a laugh I say, "That makes me feel so much better."

This woman. She's everything. So many things I didn't know I was missing. I drop a kiss on the back of her knuckles. "We're going to have a lot of fun."

She grins. Wickedly. "Yes, we are."

# CHAPTER FIFTY-TWO

## ANDRE

Gliding on an updraft, a red hawk circles lazily above the valley floor. I'm envious of its simple life. Once upon a time mine was like that.

"Hey, man. Up for company?"

I glance over my shoulder. Mako has a glass bottle of beer in his hand and his navy blue tie pulled loose beneath the collar of his dress shirt.

"Sure."

He sits on the bench with me, stretches his legs out, and sighs. "Great wedding. You enjoying yourself?"

Me? Not so much. "I'm happy for them. They've been through a lot. It's really great that they have worked things out."

"Well, you should be proud that you drove them out of that gun fight and everyone lived. "

## CHAPTER 52

"It was hairy there for a few minutes. I'm glad it turned out like it did."

"They're great together. Simona's so intense. Interesting how Scotch is the perfect balance to that. He makes her laugh all the time. And she adores him, of course."

"They seem to be having a great day."

"Hell of a party, but I couldn't resist coming to check out this view."

"This area is pretty spectacular. Going to be a nice place for them to live."

"You plan on sticking around Eden Valley for a while?"

Isn't that the question of the hour. The very one I've been pondering.

I sip off of the beer that I got at the open bar. "Not sure. It's kind of slow for me, honestly. Not the job, it's great when we're traveling, but the pace around here is a little quiet."

He chuckles softly. "Not a good place for single nightlife, you mean?"

I swallow the beer and let it slide slowly down behind the rock I have inside of my chest where most people have a heart. "Wouldn't know."

"Awe, come on, man. I'm sure you've had the urge to go out and make the acquaintance of some lovely little Utah women."

I shake my head. "Honestly, no. This wedding is the closest I've been to a group of single women in a long, long time."

"Speaking of, Simona's sisters are quite the sight for sore eyes."

"They're pretty. That's hard to miss."

His face is full of disbelief, as waves his beer around. "That's it? Pretty? How about smoking hot? And those accents. Wow. I mean, I'm just gonna say, I can imagine getting naked with one of them real easy."

I finish my beer. Silence expands between us as the hawk soars across the sky again. Faint sounds of laughter and music catch the wind and float to us from the reception. "Maybe you should see if you can make that happen."

A devious grin lights his face. "Simona would shoot me."

How true that statement is. "Yep. There's a good chance of that." I find myself scrubbing my hand over my face for the tenth time in the last hour. My mood must be obvious because his voice tone changes. "What's up with you?"

I glance back at the wedding party. "You ever just have those moments where everything hits home. The reality of how fucked up your life is lands right in your lap and there's no more denying it?"

His tone is serious, "Oh, sure. All the time. But the only way to change that is to fix what's busted up and move on."

Placing the empty bottle on the ground next to the bench, I mutter, "It would be nice if it were that simple." Looking out over the valley at the place where Simona and Scotch are going to have their new home makes me admit ugly shit to myself.

Some things are never going away no matter how much I wish they would. And that makes a mess out of everything.

"You want to get married?"

I dig my finger and thumb into the bridge of my nose. Mako's staring at me, I can feel it. "Why do you ask that?"

"People who want to be married get this weird energy around weddings."

I cut him a side eye.

He goes on anyway. "You and Marshall, man. Both of

you look like you're about to bury someone. Of course, he did get stood up at the altar, so there's that."

I shake my head. He does have a point. I'm not exactly the life of the party at the moment. "Well, I guess I have something to be grateful for. I've never been to the alter, and honestly, I'm pretty sure that's never going to happen."

Laughing, he says, "Whatever. Big ripped guy like you, all dark and dangerous. Women dig that. I'm sure you'll catch a pretty little bride one day."

When I turn to look at him his expression drops. The humor evaporates.

"Women don't love men like me. My baggage is a deal killer. Plus, I can't do the mushy shit women like, I'm not cut from that cloth."

He sips his beer. "I don't buy that anything is a deal breaker. Well, unless you're a serial killer or something."

Or something...

The hawk soars silent along on the current.

Songbirds and wind fill the air as ugly, devastating memories of my last deployment fill my head.

Mako taps his fingers against his bottle to some rhythm in his head. After a few minutes, he says, "Are you heading out of town since the Agile Team is taking some downtime?"

"Yeah. Going to D.C. to see a friend."

He pushes up off the bench. "That's good. And hey, man, if you ever want to talk, I'm happy to listen."

I tip my chin his way. "Appreciate that."

But, I won't be dishing to Mako. I've said enough already. The fewer people who know about the kind of things in my head and in my past, the better.

Details like that serve no one. Including me.

"You going somewhere?"

"Depends on how today goes."

"I thought you were worried about Simona shooting you."

"Maybe she doesn't have to know."

"You do know you're talking about a spy."

"And who knows, maybe her sister is really good at keeping secrets too." He's laughing as he strides away with a look of determination in his eyes.

Yes. Getting away from the team and from Eden will be good.

If only I could get away from myself, that would be even better.

I lurch off the bench and stride toward the party on the lawn with the intent of saying my goodbyes. It's the least I can do. I need to get out of here, because looking at pretty women only makes me feel one thing—broken.

+++

**Thank you so much for reading Dr. Trouble.**

Would you like read the 6 month & 12 month Epilogue for Scotch & Simona? Get the **bonus chapter** when you join my newsletter.

Book 3 in this series, Off-Limits Protector (Andre's book), is coming soon! Preorder today to get it when it releases in just a few weeks.

You can also get updates by texting the word **ALPHAS** to **855-256-3324**

If you fell for the characters in this book then you will love book 1, Soldier - Cole & Sierra's Story?

Check out my other books in Also By section below.

## ALSO BY JENNA GUNN

**Agile Security & Rescue Series**

Soldier - Cole & Sierra's Story
Dr. Trouble - Scotch & Simona's Story
Off-Limits Protector - Andre & Willow's Story
Marshall's Story- To Be Announced
Wolf's Story- To Be Announced

**The Eden Mountain Firefighters Series**

Saving Sophia - Liam and Sophia's story
Saving Skye - Larson and Skye's story-
Saving Summer - Carter and Summer's story
Saving Savannah - Caleb & Savannah's story
Mr. & Mrs. Strong's Story - To Be Announced

**Archer Brother's Series**

Boss Rules- Bryce and Raven's Story
Faux-Ever Rules- Christian and Maddy's Story
Broken Rules- Brandon and Anya's Story
Do-Over Rules- Bishop and Mia's Story
Friend Rules- Tyson and Abby's Story
Also available as a 5 Book Box Set on Kindle Unlimited-

Lifeguards of Lynn's Cove

**Standalone Books**

Rocked- Gage, Julian & Winter's story

Reno & Maria's story- To Be Announced

Not Over You- Anthology Collection Book (Amazon, Nook & Apple)

Risky Hero

Stella's Christmas Rescue

One Fake Night- A Valentine to Remember

Get updates on Jenna Gunn's new releases, book sales, and free books.

Join her newsletter HERE

Jenna's Facebook Group HERE

Sign Up for Text Updates by texting the word **ALPHAS** to **855-256-3324**

www.jennagunn.com

Printed in Great Britain
by Amazon